MURDER CREEK

— AN EVE SAWYER MYSTERY —

Books by Jane Suen

Children of the Future
Murder Creek

FLOWERS SERIES
Flowers in December
Coming Home

ALTERATIONS TRILOGY
Alterations
Game Changer
Primal Will

SHORT STORIES
Beginnings and Endings: A Selection of Short Stories

MURDER CREEK

— AN EVE SAWYER MYSTERY —

JANE SUEN

MURDER CREEK

Jane Suen books are available for order through Ingram Press Catalogues

www.janesuen.com

Printed in the United States of America

First Printing: June 2019

Paperback ISBN: 978-1-951002-00-8
Ebook ISBN: 978-1-951002-10-7
Audiobook ISBN: 978-1-951002-01-5

For my loved ones

Author's Note

Inspired by a road sign, "Murder Creek," in Alabama,
this book is a work of fiction.

Chapter 1

PEOPLE HAD TOLD me I have a sixth sense, and I was a good judge of character, despite my age. I couldn't describe it, but I guess I was just born this way, along with my heightened senses. I wouldn't say I could read peoples' minds, but I relied on my senses, and I focused my attention on them, just like people hone in on other skills. I believed trusting my senses had saved me on a number of occasions, and possibly saved my life. I think people might have dismissed me, wrongly so, but they did not account for my special skills and abilities—ones I didn't flaunt.

It was rare for me to idle away a day. On one such beautiful day, I took a drive, a long one crossing the state line. The flashes of sunlight danced across the windshield, patterns slipping through the trees as they streamed by. I loved it. If I had a convertible, I'd have the top down, the wind blowing my hair while the radio was cranked way up along with my voice. It was that kind of day.

I was having too much fun in my old comfortable sedan. Not a worry in the world. I was in college and working a part-time job. I was young, carefree, and I had enough to get by—I always managed if money got tight. I didn't know where I got my carefree genes. My mom was the opposite, always worrying about something. Mostly about me, I reckoned. She worried so much two furrowed lines marred her forehead right between her eyes. I didn't even think she realized what she was doing. Me, I turned out the opposite. I was bound and determined not to have those furrow lines.

Murder Creek. I gasped when I saw the sign wedged in the ground right before the bridge. The road narrowed up ahead, where it looked like two lanes were merging into a narrow bridge, so I slowed down.

I sucked in my breath. The hair prickled on my neck. As my car crawled over the wooden planks, I gripped the steering wheel and pressed my chest against it. I wanted to go faster, but my foot would not oblige. For a moment as I crossed over the creek, I felt a strange sensation, odd in ways I couldn't explain. I forced myself to look straight ahead, not down at the water. I made it almost all the way across the bridge before I dared to look quickly to the left, barely glimpsing the water's edge before the tires hit solid road again.

I didn't speed up, all the while looking for more signs, anything to provide more information. What horrific murder took place at the creek? Why was the murder immortalized?

I looked back at the sign on that side of the bridge. The same two words, Murder Creek.

Chapter 2

DRIVING WAS DIFFERENT now. No longer lulled almost to sleep, I was alert to other road signs, but there were none. The farther away I got from Murder Creek, the more agitated and restless I became. Who got murdered? When? What happened? Why?

I had questions but no answers. I seized on this puzzle, unable to let go. I couldn't wait to get home to fire up my computer.

I hit the pedal, driving as fast as I could, sometimes going a few miles over the speed limit until I arrived home. My tires screeched to an abrupt stop before turning into my driveway.

"Infamous," "historical," "robbers," and "murderers hanged," scrolled up on my Internet search. There was more than one Murder Creek. One stood out, a bloody incident at Murder Creek occurring almost two hundred years ago at the location where I crossed the bridge. To this day, questions remained about the brutal murders that took place there in the 1800s. Even the exact date in history was undetermined.

I sighed, my curiosity temporarily satiated. I got up and made a fresh pot of coffee and filled my mug.

The caffeine perked me up again. I glanced at the open page on my laptop with the photo of the creek and a map. I scrolled up to the search bar. I typed in variations of those words, "Murder Creek,", and clicked the search button for "murdered at the creek," "murder in the creek," "creek murders," and "bloody murder creek" to see what else would pop up.

It wasn't a picture of a creek this time. My heart almost skipped a beat when the photo of a beautiful young woman appeared. She was smiling, her thick long hair tousled by the wind, a few strands blowing on her cheek. Her right hand was raised, the slim fingers reaching to fetch those stray hairs. She had on a skimpy blue top with spaghetti straps, the kind you'd wear on a hot day, and white short-shorts. Her name was under the photo, Lacey Walken. I scrolled down to read the text. It was brief, a few paragraphs about a missing woman. The words "Murder Creek" ran in the sentence. She was nineteen.

Staring at her picture, I wondered what might have happened to her twenty years ago. I cursed my morbid curiosity of death and crime.

Chapter 3

MIDWAY COLLEGE WAS on the outskirts of the city. Set back from the main thoroughfare, one had to drive down a long, winding road ending in a circular drive. A series of red brick buildings clustered around the center between manicured lawns, all within easy walking distance of each other. My journalism class was in Grand Hall. I stopped by to see if my teacher, Professor Reynolds, was in his office. He answered my knock in his gruff voice, telling me to come in.

He was dressed casually in an open shirt and jeans. A jacket was flung over the spare chair. I recognized it as the only jacket he ever wore to class. Professor Reynolds was sharp, but clueless, when it came to fashion. He preferred to wear jeans day in and day out.

"Have a seat," he said, gesturing to the only empty chair.

I sat down and zipped open my backpack. I pulled out the article and waved the paper, shaking it. "She's missing!"

He looked puzzled, a bit unsettled. I suspected it was something about my voice, the emotion. I had disturbed his peace.

"Here." I shoved the paper across his desk until the picture of Lacey Walken was under his nose.

He picked it up and read it quickly. "This doesn't say much."

"You're darn right," I said. My voice was getting higher-pitched and louder.

"What's this got to do with you?"

"I want to know who she was, how she went missing, and why."

"Why are we talking about this?"

"I'm here to ask for an extension," I said, lowering my voice. "For my class assignment."

"Your report is due in a week. You're responsible for completing it if you want to pass this course."

"Hear me out, please. I'm asking you to consider giving me an incomplete and let me have time to research and investigate this." I wanted him to know I was serious and had given it some thought. "I'm going down there, to Murder Creek. I can't do it during the semester, but summer's coming up, and school will be out."

"I gave you a semester to work on this, but you're telling me this now, at the last moment?"

"I've finished my assignment, but it's not the story I want to write," I said. I pulled out my report, the one I thought boring. I implored, more determined than ever. "Please give me a chance to work on this. All I want is this summer, and you'll have your report before school starts in the fall."

"Do you feel that strongly about it?"

"Yes, sir, I do. I know there's a story." My eyes were

intense, my jaw clenched. "I'm going after it."

He leaned back in his chair. He looked thoughtful and frowned.

I kept my mouth shut. I didn't want to push it too much, or mess this up and lose my chance. I looked at the old clock on the wall, following the second hand as it moved. I knew they gave incomplete grades when there was a good excuse, often because of illness or some unforeseen circumstances beyond the student's control. I had given no assurance it would be a better story. Just my instinct and something else—a pull, a connection—something I couldn't explain, but I sensed it.

"What you're asking is highly unusual. Frankly, you're hanging your hat on a story you don't even have," he said. "My first inclination is to say no." He spread his fingers on the desk, then tapped the wood.

I gulped. I'd never been so sure of anything in the short twenty years of my existence.

"But I admit I am curious about the outcome and your insistence. What kind of story will you have? Is your journalist's instinct newsworthy?" He stopped tapping, his finger in midair, as if a thought flashed across his mind.

I sat up straight in my chair.

"Normally I'd say no, as I rarely allow these extensions. However, I have a friend, Mike Deen, who lives there. I'm thinking of making an exception in your case. He could be a contact and a resource for you, Eve."

"I'd like nothing better, Professor Reynolds," I said, more determined than ever to find the truth.

"I will give you this chance, if you're up to the challenge."

I thanked him profusely. I almost tripped over the chair in my haste to rush out of his office before he could change his mind.

Chapter 4

THE NEXT WEEK and a half sped by. I finished work on my classes, took finals, and completed the semester. All except for this one incomplete class. I focused on what I needed to do.

It was Wednesday noon by the time I was ready to leave. Murder Creek was a two-and-a-half-hour drive. I packed a few things and threw them into the back of my car. I didn't plan on staying long. I knew no one down there, but Professor Reynolds had given me a name, Mike Deen, someone I could contact in nearby Carlton, the closest small town.

I had my files with me, a few thin folders from online articles and research I did in the library. The stuff was sketchy. I didn't have much to go on.

I turned on the radio, switching channels between the news and Southern rock, to bluegrass, to country. I settled on country music. As I passed through one town and on to the next, I adjusted the frequency on the radio.

A gas station came into sight before I drove into Carlton. It had a single, wide-bay auto repair garage on one side and the gas station on the other which had a few shelves of items to buy—the usual snacks, drinks, headache powder, and car products. The guy behind the counter watched me. I looked around for the coffeepot. It was half full, and the temperature was lukewarm when I touched the carafe. It looked murky and stale. I turned around, marched to the counter to pay, and handed the man a twenty-dollar bill. "I'd like twenty on number three please."

"Anything else?"

"No," I said. "But I'll be looking for a place to say in Carlton."

The man grunted. "There's a Motel 5 down the road some. For a town this size, that's it unless you want to stay at the small boutique inn." He stared at my clothes and then at my ratty old car outside.

"As long as it has clean sheets and a decent bed," I said, smiling. "I'm not picky."

"When you get done pumping the gas, just head on down about half a mile. You'll see it."

"Thanks." I pushed open the glass door, noticing the fingerprints and grime on it.

It was a short drive to the motel, just like the man said. It had seen better days. The rickety sign needed a fresh coat of paint. Weeds poked their way up between the cracks of the walkway. I pushed open the door. Nobody was in sight. I hit the desk bell, jumping at the sharp ding. I looked around while I waited. I noticed a small sign: Free breakfast. I perked up, making a mental note to ask the clerk about the menu.

A back door opened and a scraggly-looking man walked out. "Help you?"

"I'd like a room."

"How many nights?"

"Well, I'm not sure how long I'll be staying, but I'd like to book two nights first."

The man peered at a binder behind the counter. He looked up and clicked on the computer keyboard. His ears looked large on his head. "If you need a room for this Friday or the weekend, I'll need to know the day before."

If I stretched my imagination, I might see the place in its better days. I would have bet most of their rooms were empty. The man probably was about to light up the "Vacancy" sign soon. "How much for one night?"

"Twenty-two, and with tax and all, it comes out to twenty-four dollars and ninety-nine cents."

I reached in my pocketbook and pulled out three twenties. "I'll take two nights."

He handed back the change and my room key. He pointed. "Go down that way."

I looked at my key, 105, and headed to my room.

A few steps out, I turned around. "Oh, and I almost forgot to ask about your breakfast." I glanced at the sign. My favorite meal of the day.

"Donuts and coffee."

That figured. A hot breakfast would have been too good to be true.

He said, "Remember to let me know early if you will stay. We won't have no vacancies this weekend."

"You'll be filled up?" I asked.

He nodded. "Funeral this weekend."

Chapter 5

IT WASN'T ANYTHING to write home about. I checked out my low-budget motel room. A TV, a worn chair and round table, a distressed chest of drawers, a small nightstand, and a queen-size bed draped by fading covers. I half expected to see a full-size bed, but from what I'd seen of motels bare on furniture, a queen bed as the centerpiece made up for it.

I tossed my stuff on the chair and sat on the bed. I bounced on it a few times to see if it squeaked. Oh yeah, I lucked out on this one.

My stomach grumbled, a reminder it had been a long time since I ate. I studied the flyer I took from the front desk, a map of the area. Downtown was within walking distance.

I dug up Deen's number and called. He suggested we meet at Mel's Diner, which was right down the street.

I got to the diner first and waited at the entrance. I had described what I was wearing, a white, sleeveless top and blue jeans. My sunglasses perched on my head of thick tawny hair. Bold crimson toenails pushed their way through my open sandals.

I watched him approach. I'd say he was about six feet tall, on the thin, muscular side. Probably in his late thirties or early forties. I wasn't a good guesser when it came to a man's age.

"Ms. Sawyer?" He gave a slight bow as he greeted me. I thought, *Who does that these days?*

"Yes, and you must be Mr. Deen," I said.

His handshake was firm, not clammy even on a summer day. His blue eyes reflected a calm, like a deep blue sea.

"You can call me Eve," I said and smiled, revealing my perfect teeth. My parents had paid a fortune for orthodontists, and I would flaunt my assets.

"Ladies first," he said, opening the door.

The chilled air hit me in the face. The fans were working hard overhead, and the AC was on. It must have been sweltering in the kitchen.

At barely four in the afternoon, we were early for dinner, and we had the place to ourselves. The waitress came right away and seated us at a square table against the window. She took our drink orders. I said iced tea, and Mike said he wanted the same.

"So, Eve, what brings you out here?" He got right down to business. No small talk, nothing about the weather.

"Professor Reynolds fill you in?"

"Vaguely. But I want to hear it from you."

I slid my sunglasses off and set them down carefully on the table. "I came here to do research for a class paper on Murder Creek and the missing woman, Lacey Walken."

"You want to know what happened to her?"

"I couldn't find much in the newspapers. Thought it'd be best to come here." I sighed.

The waitress brought our iced teas, then whipped out a pad tucked in her apron pocket and snatched the pen from behind her ear. "Y'all ready to order?"

"What do you recommend for a vegetarian?"

"Ma'am, the veggie plate is good. We make them fresh here. None of that canned stuff."

I scrutinized the list on the menu. "I'll have the fried okra, mashed potatoes with butter and sour cream, and mac 'n cheese please."

"I'd like two chili dogs and French fries," said Mike.

After the waitress took our orders and left, I unzipped my backpack and took out the files. I opened the one on the top. "Here's the article with her picture." I quoted the byline and summarized the contents in the brief paragraphs. "Lacey Walken did not come home. Her roommate reported her missing after her place of employment called the next afternoon, asking why she didn't show up for work. The sheriff's office questioned her and put out a missing persons alert."

"That's the picture in the newspaper."

"You were here when it happened?"

"Yes."

Mike gave me an overview of the small town here and described what Carlton was like back when Lacey disappeared. Our conversation drifted to how he had met Professor Reynolds in college. They had kept in touch on and off in the years afterwards, so when he got the call about me, he was glad to be of help.

Our food arrived just then, so I shoved my papers back in the backpack. I had a ton of questions for Mike but held off getting started when our food came. I hadn't realized how hungry I was until I took my first bite of the mac 'n cheese. It was the real thing, thick and creamy, the cheese so gooey it stuck to my fork. It really hit the spot. I stabbed the fried okra with my fork and wolfed down the rest of my food, cleaning the plate.

Mike was watching me as he took bites of his chili dog. He didn't interrupt. I thought of telling him I had skipped lunch, but he could see how ravenous I was from the way I scarfed down my meal.

I pushed my plate away when I finished. Mike was a fast eater too, and I didn't have to wait long for him.

"Good food?"

"My kind of place," I said.

He grinned. "The best place to get a home-cooked meal."

I was feeling better now with my tummy full. I can be a bitch sometimes when I'm hungry.

I welcomed the intrusion as the waitress came by to clear the table. I piled my fork on my plate and threw my napkin on top. She fussed over Mike a bit, then asked us if we wanted dessert. I had a sudden hankering for ice cream.

"What ice cream flavors do you have?"

"Vanilla, chocolate, and strawberry," she said.

I should have guessed. I'm a gal who likes chocolate, so it was an easy choice for me. Mike said to make it two.

"Mike, could you take me there?" I said after the waitress took our orders and left.

"Where?"

"For starters, I'd like to go see Murder Creek. You know, where it happened."

"You might want to change your shoes and put on something more comfortable."

"I brought a pair of boots. How far is it?"

"It's close to here. When would you like to go?"

"Bright and early in the morning."

Chapter 6

I HAD A sleepless night, waking up several times. Horrific images of a bloodbath and killing at Murder Creek, the one occurring almost two hundred years ago.

I was expecting to see Mike at eight in the morning. I was checking my phone when I heard the knock. He was right on time.

Warm humid air flowed in when I opened the door. It was early, but the cool night air had already become warmer and moisture-laden. It was the cusp between spring and summer when the flowers, watered by the April rain, bloomed in May, their roots firmly planted in soil that's rich and moist, their faces poking toward the blue sky. They hadn't encountered the summer drought or the harsh merciless rays of the sun yet. This was my favorite time of the year.

Mike was standing outside, dressed for the trek in his T-shirt, shorts, and boots. He had showered recently, and his hair still showed traces of dampness, strands clinging together.

"Ready to go?" Mike said.

I gathered my files in my backpack and closed the door behind me. I followed Mike to his truck, a big-ass shiny pickup parked in front of my motel room. He opened the door for me. I got in and noticed two coffee cups on the console and a brown bag.

"I picked up breakfast biscuits made fresh at the diner," Mike said, noting my stare. "I got you two egg biscuit sandwiches. Hungry?"

I wasn't fully functional before I had my first coffee. "Sure, thanks," I said. I reached for the egg biscuit sandwich, grateful Mike remembered I didn't eat meat.

Mike drove with the practiced ease of someone used to eating and driving at the same time. He kept his eyes on the road, with one hand on the wheel and the other holding his breakfast, or gulping coffee to wash it down.

My biscuit was perfect. The layers were flaky and buttery, the top crust browned perfectly just the way I liked it. I took my time and relished each bite.

Finished with my breakfast, I grunted in satisfaction, settling back into my seat. "Yum, good," I said, licking my greasy fingers.

"What started this interest in Murder Creek?" Mike asked.

"I saw the Murder Creek sign driving back to the city, as I crossed the bridge," I said. "I couldn't get it out of my mind."

"You know there are other Murder Creeks, not just here. It happened a long time ago. Historians tried to piece together the story."

"They say it was a traitorous deed. Men murdered in the dark of night while they slept. Bloody, violent. Committed over gold nuggets hidden in saddlebags used as pillows." I pulled out my files and opened them. "There were missing pieces of the story, questions about what took place, even the exact date."

"But you came here anyway," said Mike.

"I'm more interested in Lacey Walken."

"They talked about it for weeks. At one point, we had so many news crews from out of town we couldn't breathe."

I could imagine the crowd descending on this small town, like vultures fighting for the best pieces.

"Day after day they encamped here. If you ran into them, they would try to get you on camera for almost anything. Even if it wasn't newsworthy, it built up the excitement, sold air-time ads, or whatever."

"Meanwhile, poor Lacey had vanished."

"Without a trace," Mike said.

"Maybe her ghost haunts Murder Creek?" I mumbled, then regretted saying it. I didn't really believe in ghosts. Besides, I was getting ahead of myself and assuming Lacey *had* died.

Chapter 7

MY BLADDER STRAINED to the max, I crossed my legs and looked for a gas station. I impatiently waggled my foot, and I tapped my fingers. I didn't know Mike well enough to tell him. I merely requested that he stop at the next gas station. We hadn't gone that far, but I knew I couldn't make it all the way to Murder Creek.

When the gas station came into view, I jumped out of the truck as soon as he pulled up to the gas pumps.

I made a beeline into the women's bathroom and locked the stall door. It wasn't clean, like I'd hoped. But then again, I wasn't looking for anything fancy, and I was grateful for a toilet. It was a cramped, small space. When I bent to pull up my pants, I bumped my head into the stall door. Ouch if that didn't hurt.

I cursed and pounded my fist on the door. I caught sight of a name scratched into the wood. Lacey. Then a drawn heart with "L W + J M" carved inside it. I touched the initials, my fingers trembling as they traced the etching.

I dug out a piece of paper from my pocketbook and

scribbled it down. Could this be the same Lacey, the Lacey Walken who had disappeared? I searched for other carvings on the door with her name, but I found no more.

This was a one-stall bathroom. I checked the outside of the door just in case, but the interesting stuff is always inside the stall.

I quickly washed my hands and walked out of the bathroom. I glimpsed the men's room on the way past and had the urge to look in there. But then I saw the attendant watching me. I snatched a newspaper and made my way to the counter to pay. I mumbled "Howdy" or something like that, then dashed out and got back in the truck.

Chapter 8

MIKE WAS WAITING for me. He had already filled up with gas and got coffee refills for both of us. As soon as he saw me, he switched on the engine. I could tell Mike was an action kind of guy and serious about getting going. He didn't dillydally.

The rest of the trip was pleasant and uneventful. I thought about this new piece of information. I wanted to check the phone book for any Walken, in case there was more than one Walken in town, and relatives of Lacey.

Mike drove for about ten minutes before he pulled off the road, following a small sign on a wooden stake with an arrow pointing. We soon saw Murder Creek where the infamous nineteenth-century incident took place. We came to a large parking area worn bare of grass by countless tires. A way ahead, some trees overhung the creek, their branches casting shadows over the rocks that jutted farther out and broke the water line.

We walked to the bank. It was quiet and peaceful, the only sounds the gurgling of the water and an occasional squawk of birds, and the usual forest noises as the insects and critters got busy with their day.

Mike was talking and walking toward a group of trees by the bank. He gestured. "This is where it happened."

I walked, almost reverently, to stand by him. I closed my eyes, mouthing a silent prayer, shivering involuntarily. Scenes flashed across my mind; blood, screams, violence, and carnage. Betrayed in their sleep by strangers, men they thought were friendly. Unsuspecting and caught off-guard. They slept without a lookout. That's how much they trusted the other men. It cost them their lives.

I tiptoed to the edge of the creek, moving toward the shade of the trees.

"And this, is this the place they found Lacey's bloody scarf?" I said, pointing to the tree with branches hanging over the rocks in the creek.

He nodded.

I touched the trunk of the tree, feeling the rough gray-brown bark. My fingers knocked the edge of a loose scale, causing it to flake off.

"So how did they know it was Lacey's?"

"She was wearing the scarf the last night she worked. They matched the blood to the DNA from hair and skin on her hairbrush."

"Who found this?"

Mike said, "Visitors. Some tourists came to this place and climbed on the rocks in the creek, posing for a photo. It almost spooked them when they came across the scarf tangled in some fallen branches by the edge of the creek, and they suspected foul play when they saw the blood on it."

I felt my skin prickle with goose bumps.

Chapter 9

MY NOTEPAD WAS filling up with a list of to-dos. In the margins, I scribbled ideas and thoughts as they popped up. I planned to talk to Lacey's old roommate.

Mike offered to take me to see the long-serving sheriff, ensconced there for so long nobody could recall how long he'd been there. His familiarity with the officer might grease some skids if I needed their help. A meeting with the sheriff was a courtesy call to let him know what I was doing.

I stopped by Motel 5 to get changed and rest for a while before Mike picked me up at two in the afternoon.

Since I had a few minutes, I pulled out the phone book from the top drawer, flipped to the back to the "W's," and searched for the name "Walken."

I found two listings. I held my pencil, poised and ready to write their names, phone numbers, and addresses. None of the names listed Lacey as the first name. I didn't expect that.

I picked up my phone and called the first number. It rang four times before someone picked up. The voice on the other end sounded faint, but I could tell it was a woman.

"Hello," I said, introducing myself, and stating the reason I was calling. "Is this Mrs. Walken, Lacey's mother?"

I heard silence on the other end and erratic breathing. Okay, that was weird. So I repeated what I said.

"I'm sorry, but I can't help you," said the woman before she hung up.

What did she just do? I made a note next to the number and added "not helpful."

The next number I called, a man answered on the second ring. I went through the same spiel and introduced myself.

He sounded somewhat confused. I could almost see him scratching his head. But he didn't hang up on me. I made an appointment to see him the next morning to talk about Lacey Walken. I hoped he would be more helpful in person than he was on the phone.

It was about three minutes before two. This time I didn't wait for Mike to knock. I stepped outside to wait for him.

Chapter 10

WE PULLED UP in front of a small brick building with a flagpole in the front. The wind was blowing; I watched as the flag unfurled in its glory. We got out and walked across the parking lot. Mike had called ahead and the lone sheriff in town was expecting us.

I saw the words "Sheriff's Office" neatly inscribed on the door. Mike held the door open for me. We walked up to the counter, then the receptionist ushered us into the back to a small room where the sheriff soon joined us. His name was Ray Moore. He had a beard and was almost bald with a graying half-rim head of hair. He had a pudge in the middle, and a stocky build. He greeted Mike warmly, and then Mike introduced me.

"So, to what do I owe this visit?" he said.

"I'm a student doing research on a project," I said. "About the missing girl from Murder Creek."

He whistled and shook his head. "That was a long time ago. You sure you want to go digging again?"

"I thought maybe you could help me."

He threw a stern look at me, like a disapproving parent. "You thought this case was a cold case?"

I squirmed, detecting a change in the wind. I managed a weak smile.

"So I'm afraid I can't divulge information on the case," said Ray.

I shrugged, doing my best to hide my disappointment.

"I suggest you stick with the facts and what's already available to the public."

I thanked him for his time, and we left.

"Where to next?" said Mike.

"Next stop, the newspaper office. I'll put an ad in the paper."

His eyes widened in bemused surprise. "Clever ... you'll get your own information."

"That's right," I said as I pulled out my notepad, penning the ad.

By the time we arrived, I had finished. Mike waited outside. I handed the girl my ad, and she counted the words and gave me an invoice which I paid. The small town boasted a twice-a-week publication. I was just in time. The ad would be in the paper tomorrow.

Chapter 11

EARLY THE NEXT morning, I went back to Murder
Creek. I drove, following the route from the day before. I
turned on the radio and heard the tail end of the weather
report. They forecasted rain in the afternoon. The sky was
already gray, dark clouds heavy and ominous. I suddenly
remembered I didn't have an umbrella. But what I wanted
to do wouldn't take long. Not long at all.

The land that was so peaceful yesterday seemed different
now in the dull light. This place, where violence occurred,
the murders committed almost two centuries past.

What happened that day so long ago? Was the evil
released still here and lurking?

I rolled the car slowly to a stop and opened the door. It
was quiet. I missed the busy chitchat of the insects. The air
was still, perhaps the calm before the storm. I walked to the
creek's edge. Now I could hear the gurgling of the water
flowing. Suddenly I shivered. I didn't know why, and I felt
a chill. I stepped away from the water, turning around.

My fingers grazed the rough bark of a tree bent over the

creek. I traced the bark, moving down the trunk to the roots on the ground. I felt for a pulse, as if I could take it. I went from tree to tree down the banks of the creek. If anyone saw me here, it would look bizarre to them, I'm sure. But I was touching the trees one by one, as if in doing so, the trees would divulge their secrets.

Chapter 12

I STOPPED AT the gas station to pick up a copy of the day's paper. I sat in my car and flipped to the advertisement page on the back. The section was barely a half page and I easily scanned it, locating my ad. It was in a good position, second column at the top. Short, but clear. They listed my phone number. I folded the paper and checked my phone to be sure it was on.

It was still early as I drove back to town. I jerked, heart thumping inside my chest when I suddenly realized I had forgotten to reserve a room for the weekend. The motel clerk had warned me. I stepped on the gas, racing back.

The motel clerk was at the counter with another customer, finishing up paperwork with a middle-aged man in a tan shirt.

I walked up to the clerk when my turn came. "Good morning," I said.

"Checking out?"

I shook my head.

A flicker of irritation crossed his face. He scowled, clearly displeased with me.

31

I ventured an apology. "I'm sorry I didn't give you a heads-up. I'd like to stay the weekend ... if you have a room."

His fingers clicked on the keyboard as he stared intently at the monitor. "I'm afraid we have no vacancies."

My heart sank. "So, nothing available," I said. I reached for my pocketbook, fumbling for my room key to go pack up.

He paused, seeing my distress, and faced the screen again. "Let me check one more time."

I held my breath and crossed my fingers.

"Ah, I have you now," he finally said. "You're good to go, and you can stay in your room." I thought I detected a sneer behind his uneven, toothy grin.

I sighed with relief. "Oh, great."

"But it'll cost you more."

"How much more?"

"This weekend it'll be thirty dollars," he said, adding quickly, "I *told* you we'd be filled with the funeral and all."

I plunked down my money. "I'll take it. Thank you."

I felt relieved to get this done, expecting a busy day ahead of me. I snatched a cup of coffee and a donut on my way out. When I reached my car, my phone rang.

I took the call.

"Is this Eve, Eve Sawyer?" said a man's voice, sounding muffled.

"Speaking," I said, digging for the notepad and pen in my pocketbook.

"Uh, I saw your ad." He paused.

"Oh yes," I said, hardly able to contain my excitement.

"Well, I'm just wondering … how come you're asking about her."

"I'm doing research for a school project."

"Yeah, but why her?"

"I'm intrigued. Lacey Walken disappeared without a trace, and they matched her blood to the blood-stained scarf at Murder Creek."

"You know the sheriff has investigated this," he said.

"Do you have information for me? I'm assuming that's why you called."

"I'm warning you. Drop it now." He suddenly shouted, "Get out of town!"

The line went silent.

"No!" I cried as he cut me off. I checked the time on my phone. It was a quarter to eleven.

Chapter 13

I HATED BEING rattled, especially when I hadn't had my morning java. I sat in my car and ate my donut. It tasted stale and caught in my throat, making it hard to swallow. I washed it down with the weak motel coffee, taking long gulps. It was probably some no-name brand, but I wasn't complaining. I felt a surge of energy from the sugar rush.

Moving on to the task at hand, I picked up my phone and typed in the address for my meeting with the Walken man at eleven.

The map on my phone displayed a short five-minute drive. I could have walked from downtown. The directions led me to a house at the edge of town, and I was early.

He was waiting for me, standing on the porch. His tight lips and a faint scowl sent out unfriendly vibes. I detected a whiff of displeasure and his eyes were both curious and cold.

I jumped out of my car and slammed the door. He didn't move. I hesitated, since he had offered no greeting. I shrugged, moving the straps of my backpack up. I took a deep breath and walked toward him. The walk that said I'd take no prisoners, and I was in control.

"Eve Sawyer," I said, coming face to face with him.

He shifted slightly. A slight nod of acknowledgement.

I could tell he would not make it easy for me. "Mr. ...?"

"Amos," he mumbled. "Amos Walken."

"Any relation to Lacey Walken?"

"Yeah, a distant cousin."

"You knew her well?"

"She was a little younger than me, but heck, yes."

"What can you tell me about her disappearance?" I asked, looking at Amos. Up close I could see wrinkles on his sun-browned face, forehead, and around his eyes, the laugh lines etched around his mouth. He was chewing something, a wad tucked in his cheek.

He spat out a stream of brown tobacco juice and wiped his mouth with the back of his hand. "Done talking about that." His expression had a "I'm not going there again" look.

"How about you tell me something about growing up with her? What was she like really?"

"Lacey? Hell, she was the purtiest girl in town."

From her picture in the newspaper, I could easily see how she could be.

"All the guys were after her?"

He tugged his thumb in his jeans. "You could say so."

"Did she have someone special?"

"Not that I knew of." He sniffed and kept chewing.

"What about her girlfriends?"

"The girls were jealous of her, but she had a roommate."

I took out my pad and pen, flipping to a blank page. "Her name?"

"Sally."

"Is she still around?"

He straightened up and stared at me. Then he leaned back against the porch beam and chewed on his tobacco.

"Depends. She ain't right," he said.

"You mean she's sick?"

He shook his head. "She's half drunk, most days."

"I'm sorry, but I need to talk to her."

"I don't know if she'll want to talk to you."

I flipped my notepad to the page where I had written the two addresses. "Tell me where she lives."

He squinted, and I waited for his response. He hesitated, as if he was struggling to decide how much to say. When he finally gave it to me, I wrote it down, my fingers trembling.

I closed my pad and turned to go. "Thank you," I said, my feet bouncing down the steps.

Chapter 14

THE GPS HAD me driving past the town, ending at a destination on the other side. I hadn't realized the town extended far. Here I saw dilapidated houses, cracked sidewalks, and a run-down, weary appearance. I parked and walked to a small clapboard house needing more than a coat of paint. This was a far cry from the other side of town. I gingerly stepped on the wooden steps, testing to be sure they could hold my weight, holding the guardrails for support. I didn't see a doorbell, so I knocked on the door. The glass panes rattled as I knocked a second time, harder.

I heard a faint sound inside, a scraping noise. I held my hand over my eyes and peered through the glass, but all I could see was a dark hallway.

I waited a few more minutes and was about to leave. At the click of a lock turning, I whipped around, alert, watching the door slowly open a crack.

"Hello, I'm Eve Sawyer," I said, smiling. "I just talked to Amos Walken."

The door opened wider; the hinge squeaking. I stuck my

toes in the gap. "Are you Sally?" I paused. "I just need to talk to you for a few minutes. May I come in?"

"What do you want?" the woman croaked, her words slurred. I could see the cotton gown she was wearing. It was rumpled as if she'd slept in it.

"I'm sorry, did I wake you?" I stepped back now. I needed to gain her trust. "I just have a few questions about Lacey Walken."

"What's it to you?"

"I'm a student doing research on a term paper on the disappearance of Lacey, and I'm hoping you can help me. Were you Lacey's roommate?"

She gave a throaty laugh, then hacked a cough. "Yeah, until she disappeared and stiffed me with the rent."

"But someone could have forced her, taken her against her will."

She was quiet. Like her mind had cleared for a moment. "I don't believe that."

"Why?"

"She took her gold locket."

"How would you know?"

"I searched for it afterwards. I was desperate for money, and I thought I could ... you know, sell it." She looked at me, unashamed. "A girl's gotta do what she's gotta do."

"Are you sure Lacey had it?"

"I knew where she kept it in her room. It was hidden, shoved in the back of her dresser drawer."

"She told you about that?"

Sally shook her head. "I went through her clothes once,

38

looking to borrow a top. I reached back in the drawer and my fingers touched something small and hard, a jewelry box."

"You've never seen Lacey wear it?"

"Nope, she never showed it to me either. I sneaked a peek and saw the gold locket inside."

Chapter 15

I DROVE BACK to the motel to take a quick nap.

I tossed everything on the table, including my pocketbook, and went to the bathroom. Running the water from the sink, I washed my hands and splashed water on my face. I felt tired suddenly, as I flopped on the bed.

My phone woke me up. It wasn't a grouchy wake-up where I hadn't had enough sleep. I don't know how long I slept, but I felt satisfied, refreshed. I reached for my phone. It was Mike.

"Hello," I said, rubbing my eyes, and I yawned.

"Hey, how's it going?"

"It's been interesting."

"Are you staying or leaving today?"

"I'm here for the weekend."

"Want to meet me for dinner?"

I checked the time. It was four thirty in the afternoon. "Sure, what time?"

"Thirty minutes, at the diner?"

"Okay." I ended the call, running to the bathroom.

Chapter 16

WHILE I'D SLEPT, the dark clouds had churned, and the promised rain came, covering everything with a wet blanket, but it didn't wake me. I was so tired. I had learned a few things about Lacey, things not reported. The photo haunted me, the face of Lacey. I refused to believe her life had been extinguished. A part of me wanted to find her alive, to search for her. But I also knew it might be hopeless. Others had tried, and the trail had gone cold.

I considered the possibilities, conjecturing on what could have happened. I pulled back the faded orange-brown curtains, revealing the still-cloudy day. Raindrops had splattered the windowpane, leaving translucent tails streaking down the glass. My stomach growled, reminding me I hadn't eaten since this morning, the stale donut long gone.

The rain had quieted down to a soft drizzle. I gathered my backpack and left, closing the door behind me. I walked to the diner despite the rain.

The windows were fogged from the humidity. I went inside quickly, feeling assured of having someone to talk to, someone who I trusted.

Chapter 17

I FOUND MIKE at a table, back from the windows this time. I waved and went over. He hadn't ordered yet.

"Hi, Mike," I said.

He jumped up and pulled out a seat for me.

I nodded a thank you.

The same waitress came by and took our orders. I asked for the same plate of vegetables. Mike had an eight-ounce steak, with a baked potato slathered with butter and sour cream. It'd been so long since I'd had meat that the smell of it made me sick. I said nothing though and concentrated on my meal.

Mike was looking at me with a bemused expression as I wolfed down my food. I told him I was hungry, having skipped lunch. I ordered a slice of apple pie to satisfy my sweet tooth.

"So, tell me more about you." I said, turning my full attention to Mike.

"What do you want to know?"

"How d'you end up here?"

"My mama fell in love with a northerner. When they got married, she left with him and they moved back up north. Then I came along." He chuckled.

I smiled.

He paused, his face all serious. "When Dad died after an accident, Mama moved back home. Mama didn't like the weather up there. It was cold, especially where they lived in the Dakotas. She never got used to it."

"Your mama …"

"She loved her husband. When he died, the spark went out of her and she was never the same afterward."

"She had you."

"She raised me," said Mike. "At night, when it was all quiet, I could hear her. She thought I was asleep. But I wasn't always. That's when she'd cry."

"I'm sorry."

"I couldn't do anything." He sighed.

"You were a child."

"I'd catch her looking at me sometimes with a dreamy look like she was elsewhere." Mike had the most forlorn look on his face. His mouth pursed tight, like he was stubborn and refused to cry. There was a hint of a quiver on his lips.

"Did you … were you like your dad?"

"She said I looked like him, my nose." He crinkled his face. "Like this."

I didn't have the heart to ask him how much of his dad he remembered. All I could do was stare at his nose. It was strong, aquiline. I noticed none of the flared nostrils and reddened veins which older men get when they'd been habitual drinkers. I stayed quiet, out of respect and because I didn't know what to say.

"How did your day go?" asked Mike after a moment of silence.

"Good, although I took a nap and slept through the rain."

"We get those a lot, the quick summer thunderstorms." He didn't banter much and came straight to the point. "Tell me what you found out today."

"I talked to a relative of Lacey's and her roommate."

Mike raised his eyebrows, but kept his mouth shut.

"It seems Lacey was popular with the guys," I said. "You've never mentioned it when we talked."

"You've never asked me that exactly."

"You knew her. What was she like?"

Mike stroked his chin and took a sip of water before he answered. "Lacey was a special girl. Sure, she was beautiful, but her beauty wasn't just skin-deep."

"Go on."

"The way I heard it, one time she found an injured bird. It was lying on the ground, and it couldn't fly. She took it to the vet," said Mike.

"She liked animals."

"She stuck up for little kids too. Word got around the time she was walking home from school and saw one of the bigger boys kicking a little kid. He had his fists up and was getting ready to pummel the kid."

"She didn't jump in the fight, did she?"

"No."

"What did she do?"

"She pulled the little kid up from the ground and sheltered him with her body," said Mike. "He was ready to punch her out. But the look she gave him …" He stopped to shake his head. "It was something fierce."

"So she was kind and vanilla sweet. Sounds boring."

"Not; she had a nasty side, like we all do. If you got on her bad list, you would endure the brunt of her anger."

"What about her parents? Were they strict on her or what?"

"She was raised by a single mom. She left home later and moved in with Sally."

"What about school?"

"She quit suddenly when she started working full-time at the pizza joint."

"They called the sheriff when she didn't show up for work?"

"Right. As they reported it, her shift at the pizza place started at four in the afternoon," Mike said.

I took out my notepad and outlined a time frame. "Did her roommate see her the night before?"

He shook his head. "I think she worked the four to twelve shift the night before. If she came home late, her roommate may not have seen her—and Sally had a day job at the grocery store. So, she wouldn't have known."

"Ah, then it makes sense," I said. "Lacey didn't show up at four, the pizza place called home, and when she couldn't be found and they discovered her bloody scarf—they reported her as missing."

"You got it."

"According to the newspaper, she disappeared sometime between midnight and four in the afternoon the next day."

Chapter 18

I DRUMMED MY fingers on the table. "Did Lacey have any enemies?"

"Not that I knew of," said Mike.

"Is the pizza place still open?"

"No, that place, the Pizza GoKing, was a hang-out for kids after school. But after Lacey went missing, it closed up."

"That's odd. Do you know why?"

"Not a clue."

I made a note to look into Pizza GoKing. "Who was her boss at the time?"

"They interviewed him on the news," Mike said. "He liked the attention, I could tell, and embellished it—the part about when she didn't show up, and what lengths he went to after that."

"His name?"

"I can't recall."

I made another note to find his name. It was getting late, and I still needed to hit the library and check out the local papers. I planned to make that stop after dinner.

It felt like a productive day. I stretched, yawning deeply. My second full day and things were happening. I jotted down all my questions on another page, all the whys and what made sense, and what didn't.

I dug into the apple pie, cutting into the scoop of vanilla ice cream. I could eat this every day.

Chapter 19

THE UNASSUMING BUILDING was set back from the road, the parking lot overtaking the front and side of the lawn. I almost didn't see it. The bronze plaque—Carlton Public Library—was the only sign on the front door. The interior reminded me of my elementary school library in the city. It was small and cozy, shelves stuffed full of books, an atmosphere of charm. The gray-haired woman at the desk looked up when I approached.

"Nice place here," I said.

She smiled warmly, the welcome you'd get when you're a frequent customer. "How can I help you?"

"I'd like to speak to the reference librarian please."

"That's me." She waved her hand at the room. "I'm the only one here today."

"I'm in luck then." I chuckled. Maybe it was the rain, but I only saw three other library users.

"You're looking for something in particular?"

"Lacey Walken. Anything about her and what happened at Murder Creek."

The librarian, wearing a name tag with "Agnes" pinned to her shirt, raised her eyebrows. She came around the counter and gestured for me to follow her. We entered a room with a table, chair, and a microfiche reader. She showed me how to use it. "We have the articles on Lacey from our local newspaper stored in the cabinets here," said Agnes, proudly.

"Thank you," I said. "Can I get print copies?"

"Yes, you'll need to pay for each copy."

"Good deal."

"Just see me before you leave. I'll get you squared away."

I settled in, dropping my backpack on the carpeted floor and flipping my notebook open. No wonder I didn't see these articles on the internet. These were local, going back several decades.

My fingers moved the guide on the reader, scrolling across and down the pages as I scanned the microfiche. Sandwiched in the local articles were a few from the major papers, having made it to the national news. I couldn't believe my luck. I saw the same name over and over, Mark Sewell, the reporter on the local articles.

I found the pizza place articles Mike had mentioned over dinner. Mike was right about the manager, whose name was Clint Madden; he sure wasn't shy. He was interviewed, but it was consistent with the timeline I had diagrammed in my notebook.

I didn't find the cousin mentioned, but they interviewed Sally the roommate. My interest piqued, I read the article, focusing on what she said, looking for the reference to the locket. There was none.

My eyes needed a break from the intense work. I found myself with my nose almost to the screen. I had to squint to read, and I felt a throbbing headache coming. I got up and stretched, walking out of the room for a breath of fresher air. There was only one other person there besides me. I ambled to the circulation desk to chat with Agnes. She was checking a stack of books in from the return slot.

"Agnes, do you have a phone book?"

She reached under the counter and pulled one out; the handwritten words "library copy" inscribed in black magic marker across the cover. "That's my only copy. Be sure you get it back to me."

I nodded my thanks. "By the way, what time do you close?"

"Today we close at seven." She looked up at the clock. "You've got twenty-five minutes."

I murmured my thanks and went back to the microfiche room, the phone book tucked under my arm.

I dialed Mark Sewell first. He answered on the second ring.

"Mark Sewell? This is Eve Sawyer."

"I know who you are," Mark said. "I figured I'd get a call from you sooner or later."

"But ... but how did you know?" I stammered. Yet a part of me thought, *It's his business to know.*

"A reporter never reveals his source."

"I'd like to meet with you. Would you have time tomorrow?"

"I'm tied up tomorrow, you know, covering the funeral."

My ears perked up, having heard the motel clerk mention this at least twice. "So who died? Some big-shot around here?"

I felt the hostility over the phone. The silence stretched.

"You need to do your research." The line clicked dead.

I jumped up and grabbed my backpack. I rummaged inside, searching for the paper. It was crumpled and shoved in the bottom. I pulled it out, laid it on the table, and smoothed it out. Whew ... how did I miss that? On top of the front page was a banner headline about the funeral. The service was scheduled at eleven tomorrow morning. I shrugged. I didn't know this person, and I was about to put the paper away when I saw, "A businessman, former owner of Pizza GoKing and other local establishments ..." There was a headshot of a stern-looking silver-gray-haired man dressed in a tailored suit. "Mr. Travis Madison III."

Chapter 20

I MADE IT a habit to pack one thing whenever I traveled—my little black dress. It had come in handy more times than I could count. It wasn't a fancy dress, just a plain one without decorations. It saved my butt many a time: when I needed a dress for dinner, even a semi-formal event, and now a funeral. I thanked God I had packed it this time. I rushed back to my motel room to look for it since I was going to the funeral. I had my good luck charm; I held the dress and hugged it, sighing with relief.

I had a feeling most of the town would be there. I was disappointed in the demise of Mr. Madison before I could talk to him. I wondered how many secrets he was taking to his grave.

I felt sad, even though I didn't know him.

I pulled out my laptop and turned it on. It was time to learn all I could about Mr. Travis Madison III. There was a lot on the Internet. He had a long life, having lived for eighty-three years. He grew up on a farm, around farming and livestock. A stocky boy, he played football well enough to get a college scholarship.

He was a shrewd businessman. Early on, he had tinkered with farm machinery and discovered he had a talent for it. He made good money fixing equipment.

Travis came up with an idea for an improvement to the seed drill, a machine which planted seeds in rows at a precise depth, preventing birds from eating the seeds or them being blown away. He eventually patented this part and a smaller-size seed drill which was more affordable.

In the early years, he traveled around the country as a salesman. He worked tirelessly to build his business, a step at a time. He gave a warranty for double the number of years his nearest competitor gave. Fortune smiled on him, and a buyer placed a large order. From then on, the business really took off. Travis became a local success.

On his fortieth birthday, he had no heirs. In fact, he had no wife. Too busy to love, Travis Madison had spent the first half of his life building his business, working relentlessly day and night. Travis cultivated the image of a successful, wealthy man. There was a long line of women who wanted to be Mrs. Madison III. He spun the roulette wheel and picked a number. Literally, that's how he chose his wife. Not out of love or even lust. Travis used to joke about it when he was drunk—it was God's hand that picked his wife.

When Travis proposed to her, Chastain had quickly accepted. Their engagement photos with her sporting the enormous diamond ring were splashed across papers and magazines. He let her plan the details of the wedding. In every picture they were together they had posed, holding hands to show affection. They had two children in quick succession, both boys.

About twenty-five years later, when their marriage fell apart, the news printed devastating personal accounts by Chastain of a loveless marriage, one that fell far short of what she had expected. He'd called it a business proposition. But she had turned a deaf ear to that and only registered the words she wanted to hear. Travis came to her and did his duty. And he expected her to do hers, which was to produce heirs. The engagement ring, the wedding—it seemed all so romantic at the time, but in reality, it was a cold-hearted business deal. She had something he wanted, and he had something she wanted. Even the children knew their marriage was a facade, and the end was inevitable.

I had read quickly, fascinated by this man's story. I was curious to learn more about the man and his life.

Chapter 21

I TRIED TO sleep, but my mind stayed awake. The things I read and found out churned, tossing me until I had no peace. I didn't know how I made it through the night, but by daybreak I was ready for the day.

So many unanswered questions. It seemed the deeper I dug, the more questions I had. I didn't expect to be in this situation now. I worried about what was yet to be uncovered. But I came here for the truth, and I was more determined than ever to find it.

I washed up and applied makeup carefully. My usual was light, just a touch of gray eyeshadow and pale pink lipstick, but today I added blush and twirled my hair up in a bun, sticking in a pair of chopsticks to hold it up.

The night before, I hung my black dress on a clothes hanger, straightening out a few wrinkles. For some reason I felt nervous, not only because I don't like going to funerals, but I felt like an intruder, someone from the outside witnessing the mourning of unrelated family and their friends. A part of me was curious about this man and his hometown. According to the papers, he had a second home in the city and already had a public memorial service. This one was more intimate, in the bosom of where he was born and grew up. Back to the place he left, years ago, then returned to. His final resting place would be in a private cemetery next to his parents. Travis Madison III had planned for this and purchased the plots, enough for his entire family.

I topped my attire with a strand of pearls and walked out the door.

Chapter 22

THE CHURCH WAS probably the biggest building in town. It was painted white, a spire on the roof, a sign swinging from two chains dangling from a sturdy wooden post.

Mike was waiting for me outside, all dressed up in a dark suit. The sunlight glinted, playing hide-and-seek between his thick clumps of hair. His eyes lit up when he saw me, a bare tilt of his head in an approving nod.

"I almost didn't recognize you," I said.

"I dug out my Sunday best."

His fingers touched a button, making sure it secured the suit over his concave belly. "You look nice."

"Shall we?" I said, eager to move inside the church, which was rapidly filling. I took a program on my way in.

Mike offered his arm and steered the way to an inconspicuous spot at the far end of a pew, about three-quarters of the way from the back. He sat at the edge, and I squeezed into the empty space beside him. It was so tight we rubbed shoulders. I opened the program and glanced down to see who would be speaking. I knew from my research Travis Madison III's ex-wife had preceded him in death. His remaining heirs were their two sons, Jeremy and James.

I felt a soft jab. Mike threw a look at the first row. "The guy sitting on the left is his oldest, Jeremy. James is the younger child." Both his sons would be speaking, delivering eulogies. I figured Mike would be close in age to the two sons.

I raised my head, making a mental note of faces as Mike whispered in my ear, mentioning their names as people passed by.

When Jeremy got up to speak, the expectant silence was thick. I found myself holding my breath. He looked to be in his early forties. He had a thick, full head of hair, precisely cut. Masculine designer spectacle frames accentuated his square jaw. He spoke from a scripted speech. Quiet, dignified, and measured—the unhurried speech of someone in mourning, and used to having people hanging onto every word.

James got up after his brother finished. Strikingly handsome, he was a slightly younger version without the glasses. He lacked the smooth assuredness of his older brother. His voice cracked as he spoke, and he had to pause before he could continue. He seemed oblivious to how he looked and ran his hands through his hair in a nervous gesture. But when he got going and his voice gained tenure and strength, he dispensed with the prepared speech and instead spoke from the heart. Soft, but powerful, the words spilled out. I felt his pain, and he did not hide his tears.

The service was over in an hour. Afterwards, the family was proceeding to the burial site for a private graveside ceremony. The sunlight shone through the stained-glass windows, heavenly rays casting an ethereal glow on the beautiful flower arrangements and casket sprays. Mike's hand touched my elbow, guiding me toward the door as we left the church.

Chapter 23

MIKE INTRODUCED ME to people. I saw Agnes from the library. She was dressed in severe black mourning garb. I didn't see Sally—frankly; I didn't expect to see her here. Mike walked toward Jeremy and James, who were standing together. He gestured for me to come closer. I had fallen back, reluctant to approach the two brothers, feeling out of place. They stood next to each other, greeting each guest as they offered words of support and comfort, expressing condolences. Mike paused, seeing my hesitation.

"Please, come."

I shook my head. "No, you go ahead."

"I'd like you to meet them," he said. Mike grasped my hand and gently pulled me forward.

I found myself face to face with Jeremy. I sensed his strength, his firmness. He kept his composure and shed no tears in public, but I had a feeling he'd display his grief in the confines of his home. I shook his hand. His grip was cool and strong. I murmured my condolences, feeling helpless to do anything.

I turned to see James looking at me quizzically. He introduced himself, but I felt like I already knew him after how he'd spoken at the podium. At other times his mouth had silently moved, as if he was talking to someone unseen. But he could have been saying a prayer. I could tell he still had the shocked look. His dad hadn't been well, and although one could prepare for the end, it's never how you'd expect it. James, the younger son, had been his father's favorite, according to Mike. He wasn't all serious and businesslike, like his brother.

Travis Madison III had left his estate to both his sons. But the Palladian-style inspired home, the coveted *plume*, had gone to James. I don't know how Mike knew this, but in a small town everybody knew everybody's business, especially someone who was a pillar of the community.

James's eyes were still red. I expressed my condolences. I couldn't think of anything else to say. He shook my hand, and I moved on.

"Hey, Mike," I whispered as we walked outside. "Can you point Mark Sewell out to me?" I wanted to meet the town's reporter.

"He's over there," Mike said, nodding toward a man who stood farther out and away from the gathering, holding a cell phone to his ear.

I took a step in his direction, ready to get in his line of sight as soon as he'd finish talking. I didn't see Amos coming from my right, and I almost ran into him.

"Ms. Sawyer," he said. "I'd like to speak to you."

I turned, noting his nervous twitch on his cheeks. "Amos Walken," I said.

He was holding his hat in his hands, turning the rim around and around.

I wondered what he'd have to say this time. I chimed in before he could get the next word out. "You are just the person I want to see." It was true, and he had been on my mind.

He looked pleased.

"I've been thinking about Lacey's mother," I said. "I've tried to talk to the only other Walken in the phone book. I'm afraid I've come to a dead-end." My eyes searched his, imploring.

"There's only one Walken left. She's Lacey's mom."

I looked around the place, hoping to catch sight of her. "She's here?"

"Nope, but she'd like you to come by today," Amos said.

I was elated, of course, my brain already working overtime to come up with questions for her. She must have changed her mind—and was the woman that hung up on me when I called, before I posted the ad, before I talked to Amos. Perhaps she'd rather let things stay where they were, but not now.

"What time?"

He shrugged. "Well, I'm supposed to tell you to come after the funeral."

I pulled out my notebook and shoved it in front of Amos. "Is this where I'll find her?"

Amos squinted at my bad writing. He probably wasn't the brightest bulb in the room, but he had overcome whatever hesitancy he had from yesterday to deliver this message to me. I wondered if she was too ill or too old to attend the funeral.

"Thank you, Amos," I said before hurrying to catch up with Mark Sewell.

Mark had finished with his call and was busy scribbling on his notepad. I was trying to figure how to approach him, given his cold treatment of me yesterday. I decided I'd do my best to start over. Mark looked like he was in his late forties or early fifties, with slightly slumped shoulders and bad posture. He was a thin man and reminded me of a bird. He nervously peered at me.

I called out quickly before he could move away. I made sure I had my smile ready along with a warm "hello." "Eve Sawyer," I said, adding, "We talked yesterday, on the phone. You're Mark Sewell?"

He looked at me for a moment before he acknowledged me. I bet he remembered lots of details, names, places, and dates. A ridiculous thought popped in my head. "Bird brain." Which wasn't funny, as his head was rather large compared to the rest of his rail-thin body. He probably had a high IQ to boot. He took his time before he reached out to shake my hand.

"So we meet," I said pleasantly. "I've been reading your articles."

He grunted, shifting the phone to his back pocket. "What can I do for you?"

"If you have a few minutes, I'd like to ask you some questions." Not to sound blunt, I explained, "I'm not reporting on her story; you've already done that. I'm a student working on a class assignment about Lacey Walken. I'm doing some research—if there's anything new on this old case, what I can find out."

"And?"

"Well, you see, this beautiful woman just up and disappears, and the assumption was she was a victim of violence, judging from her bloody scarf at Murder Creek." I paused, checking his reaction. I saw a flicker of irritation. Of course, this was old news, what he had reported. "But I don't think that's what happened to her."

"You found out something?" His beady eyes were alert now, his nose for news sharpened on the hunt.

"I'm not sure. I don't know who would have the motive. Why would anyone go to all that trouble and lead investigators to the creek?"

He acknowledged it. "It was perplexing. There was no body, no trace of her apart from the bloody scarf. The search party combed the creek and along the banks for miles."

"Do you have *any* idea who would have done this?"

He snorted, shaking his head. "If you're smart, I suggest you not waste your time here."

I noticed Mike off to the side, waving, giving me a curious look. I walked away, toward him.

"Now what was that all about?" he asked.

"Never try digging for a story from a reporter," I rasped, spitting out my words and my distaste of Mr. Bird Man.

Chapter 24

I SET OUT to see Lacey's mom after the funeral. My GPS led me to a modest cottage on the outskirts of town, not far from the church. It was painted light blue, and the lawn was trimmed.

I folded my sunglasses and left them on the dashboard of my car. I straightened my dress, opened the door, and slid out.

Mrs. Walken was sitting on her porch chair, waiting for me. I could only hope Amos had put in a good word for me. She wore a thin cotton dress. Her gray-streaked hair was twirled and caught up in a loose bun. Something about the way she sat, or perhaps it was the way she held her head high, her blue eyes fixed on me, that spoke volumes of her poise and no-nonsense attitude.

I reached out to shake her hand. "Mrs. Walken," I said. "I'm delighted to meet you. I mean, Amos said to come and see you."

She grinned. "Amos, he's a good boy." She paused. "Family, you know. All the family I got left."

"Yes, ma'am," I said politely as she waved for me to take a seat.

"I hear you've been asking questions about Lacey."

I could see traces of her beauty from a long time ago. Faded now, and she knew it. I knew it because she hadn't taken care of herself or bothered to apply makeup. She didn't seem to care that I saw her face, scrubbed and bare. "I'd like to talk to you about Lacey. First, what was she like?"

Mrs. Walken sat back in her chair and closed her eyes. I could hear the birds rustling the leaves in the treetops. It sounded so far away. It was peaceful here. I sensed her life was lonely, even sad.

She seemed to read my thoughts. "You don't have to worry about me. I still miss her, you know, my Lacey." Her fingers traced the pattern of the wood on the armrest of her chair. "That child, from the day she was born, had the loudest cry. She never slept through the night like some babies do. Kept me awake." Her eyes peered into mine. "But you know, Lacey was strong. She knew what she wanted." She paused, shaking her head. "Stubborn too. I tried to talk her out of wearing that yellow dress one time, and she wouldn't hear of it."

I was all attention, hearing firsthand what Lacey was like.

"Lacey was beautiful, and she realized the power of her beauty from the time she was young."

I remembered the photos of Lacey in the newspapers. It took my breath away. I could imagine it was evident, even at that early age.

"Did she ... have any enemies?"

"Girls envied her, guys fought over her. But not enemies like that."

"Why would anyone want to hurt her?"

She fixed her eyes on me, narrowing as if she had a shrewd thought. "My baby had no enemies."

"Would she tell you if she did?"

She paused. "She had already moved out and got a job at the pizza joint. I didn't hear from her as often after that. She lived with Sally."

"I spoke to Sally, went to her place. Is that where she lived with Lacey?"

"Oh, that place, I thought they would have torn it down by now," said Mrs. Walken. "We didn't talk as much later. I'd call and asked how she was doing. Or she'd call, usually on Sunday, and chat with me for a few minutes."

"And she never said she was afraid of anyone?"

She frowned. "Not exactly. But one time she asked …"

"Ask what?"

"If she could move in here for a while," she whispered.

"And when did she say that?"

Mrs. Walken folded her hands in her lap and raised her head. "A couple of days before she disappeared."

Chapter 25

I RUSHED BACK to the motel to change. Suddenly, I felt uncomfortable in my black dress and spike heels. Maybe it was the funeral, the stuffiness of the church, or what Lacey's mother confided in me. I shimmied out of my clothes and pulled on a T-shirt, a pair of comfortable, familiar blue jeans and well-worn shoes. I tied my hair back in a ponytail and splashed warm water on my face. I used a towel to dry it and held it close, smelling the chlorine on it.

On my way out, I stopped by the motel front desk. The same clerk was there.

"I just got back from the funeral," I said, making conversation.

He grunted.

I poured coffee from the carafe, not caring if it was fresh. My head screamed for caffeine. "Did you know him?"

"Everyone did, the old dinosaur. But I didn't know him that well. He didn't exactly run in my circle." He smirked, spitting out a coarse laugh.

"What about Lacey, did you know her?"

"Yeah, but she was younger."

"Did you see her in school?"

"Until she quit going, then I hardly saw her much after that."

"Did she have any enemies?"

"Look," he said, bending over the counter, up close in my face. "I don't know what you're digging at, what you're trying to do, but I'm not her buddy."

I was taken aback by his answer and his ferocity. "She disappeared, and no one knows where. Don't you care?" Maybe there was something he wasn't telling me, something he was hiding behind the scraggly beard. "But you know something, don't you?"

"Why don't you ask your friend?"

I blinked. How did he know I was talking to Mike? He must have seen him outside picking me up. Was Mike holding back on me too?

Holding my paper cup of lukewarm black coffee, I darted out to my car. I just wanted to drive away, to anywhere but here.

Chapter 26

I TORE OUT of the motel parking lot, driving on autopilot. It didn't take long for the town to disappear from the rearview mirror. I sped across the forest toward the creek. I slowed down as my tires churned up the gravel on the country road and parked. I got out to take a walk. I headed to the tree at the edge of Murder Creek with its branches bowing over the stream. It was so peaceful here, the gentle gurgling of the water, the busy buzz of the insects getting on with their lives.

Flashes of visions popped up. Of men, laughing and joking as they gathered twigs and small branches, started a fire, prepared a meal. I saw the horses behind them, tied to other trees. I saw the day turning to dusk and the flames burning brighter. I saw more men coming closer, strange men in rough, dirty clothes asking for directions. But they weren't turned away. They sat, joining the group, and food was passed to them.

The snap of a branch jolted me back to the present. I stiffened, my senses raised to the possibility of danger. I thought I was alone.

"Sorry to disturb you," said a man's voice. I turned to look. He was dressed in a cotton shirt and slim-fit dark jeans.

James Madison.

"James, right?" I blurted out, although I knew.

"Most people call me Jim." He took a few steps closer, as if to greet me. "And you are?"

"Eve Sawyer." I held out my hand. "We met earlier today."

"Oh yes, I'm sorry. You look different."

I stood silent for a while. Maybe he wanted to be by himself, to mourn his dad's passing.

"You come here often?"

"I used to. A long time ago." He put both of his hands in his pockets. As if he needed to stabilize, to hold his feet firmly on the ground. He scuffed the dirt with his toe.

I felt uncomfortable, like I should be going. I took a step.

"Please stay," he said. "I wouldn't mind some company now."

"I'm sorry about your dad," I said. "What you said up there was heartfelt. I didn't know him, but through your words I felt your pain ... and your love."

"We all knew, the family that is, that he was ill and didn't have long to live. It wasn't unexpected. My dad was a businessman, and he made plans for it, long before." He paused and shook his head. "I guess he wanted to spare us the work. Everything was in place. All the paperwork, his will, the legal documents, the funeral, the burial plot."

"Even the words on his headstone?"

"Even that, he didn't forget anything. He was that kind

of man." Jim choked and a sob escaped from his lips. "I miss him."

"Did you get to tell him everything before he passed?"

He looked at me, hard, as if debating what I knew, what I had meant. Finally, he said, "No."

I changed the subject. I didn't know the man or what to say, really. "Did you know Lacey Walken?"

He straightened. His eyes scrutinized mine, peering suspiciously. "Why do you ask?"

I explained my school project, made it sound bland and nonthreatening. "I thought you might have known her," I said, adding lamely, "You being around the same age and all."

He closed his eyes. I wondered if he was trying to concentrate to remember, or to block out something. His eyes were an indeterminable shade of gray with specks of green. His expression pulled me, tugging me like waves, carrying me to the ocean. Then back here to the creek. Was it deep sorrow I detected? Or regret, or something else?

"Do you want to talk about it?" I said.

He wrestled with his emotions, his face twisting one way and another. Then I saw him relaxing, as if he gave up or gave in. Was he a tortured soul? More than just grief-stricken?

"Lacey?" I whispered, prodding him.

"I knew Lacey growing up. We were the same age. She was a skinny tomboy, fearless, braver than the boys she played with." He paused. "We did sprints at the elementary school. For the annual race. I won the blue ribbon in the boys' group, and she won in the girls. She had those long skinny legs … then she spurted up in her teens. I mean everywhere. She turned into a woman overnight. A beautiful one, like a goddess."

I nodded.

"It wasn't just me that noticed. Everyone did, the young and the old. She changed, too, and became less of a tomboy. We had hung out here a lot. On lazy summer days, the kids all came here to swim in the creek. Nobody minded; we all knew each other."

"But later?"

"Later we still came here, but it wasn't all innocent and fun like when we were kids." He shook his head, brushing his hair back. "Lacey would stand on that rock," he said, waving to the large flat rock. "She'd do a tease, some kind of dance wiggling her hips." He noticed the look on my face, and my eyes widening. "No, not like that, it wasn't a sexy tease. It was still childish, a natural one, something she did on the spur of the moment."

I could picture Lacey standing there, the wind blowing her long hair, the awkward wiggling of her body, dancing to a new tune.

"We were all changing and dealing with our bodies and minds. We were a group of kids who knew each other, grew up together. Sure, we played pranks on each other. What kids didn't? But if anyone outside pranked us, or tried to, we'd be together as a group. Looking out for each other."

I pictured the brothers squabbling and fighting. And still having each other's back.

"What happened to Lacey?"

Jim opened his mouth, but closed it again before speaking. Then he said, "I should tell you something else, something Lacey and I did." He struggled, his face contorting again. "I admired Lacey—no, I *loved* her. For years I watched over her, acted like the brother she never had. We were that way with each other. I grew taller, over six feet, and she had to look up at me."

"So you were like friends?"

"Yup. But it all changed one day."

I gripped the edge of my belt, leaning forward to catch his words.

"Lacey and I ..." he began. "I mean, she got a job at the pizza joint after her mom gave her a hard time and she moved out."

"To live with Sally," I said.

He sighed. "I worried about that. It was a dump of a place by the railroad tracks." He frowned. "But Lacey was stubborn. I couldn't talk her out of it."

"And Sally?"

Jim laughed, a hard, gritty sound. "She was a whore, older than Lacey."

"How did they meet?"

"They both worked at the pizza joint. Initially, Lacey was going to school full-time and working at the pizza place some evenings and weekends."

"I heard she quit school," I said.

"She couldn't make ends meet on her paltry salary and the tips. So she quit school altogether to work full time." He pursed his lips, disapprovingly or in disgust, I couldn't tell. "I couldn't talk her out of that either."

I shook my head, knowing where she had ended up.

He clenched his fist. "I tried to get her to come back to school, but she stuck her head in the sand. She wouldn't listen."

Chapter 27

"WERE YOU LOVERS?" I asked.

He didn't seem surprised. He looked at me with a sad expression.

I knew he was in love with her. Still. And he was a man in pain, even after all these years.

I added, "Did you look for her?"

Jim sighed, rubbing his still red-rimmed eyes. "After what happened here, we had search parties going for days. My father, you know he was rich ... well, he paid for people to join the search when we didn't have the local capacity to keep it going."

"He sounds like a good man," I said, thinking of the nice things people said at his funeral. No one would ever speak ill of the dead. "What did you do?"

"We followed the creek downstream and searched the banks. It was slow going, covering the distance in the forests and on both sides of the creek. We had teams going around the clock."

"Why did your dad pay for the search?"

He hesitated. "It was his way of helping."

"Did you come across anything?"

"No, we found nothing. It was like she'd vanished into thin air."

I swallowed and asked the question I dreaded. "Do you think she's dead?"

"Everyone assumed that. But I, even now, hold the hope, the slimmest of hope, that one day we'll find her." He added in a low soft tone, "May she be in peace."

Chapter 28

MY STOMACH WAS grumbling again as I drove back to town, my mouth salivating over a home-cooked meal at the diner. The waitress recognized me right away and whisked me to a corner table. Happily ensconced there, she brought me a fresh cup of coffee before I ordered my usual.

I got comfortable and spread out my notes and articles on the table, and the newspaper clipping of Lacey. I somehow wanted Lacey to know that I was just as stubborn as her. Even though they had searched high and low for her, I would not give up. I was determined, now more than ever. Digging for little crumbs as best as I could. Hoping the pieces would come together. But right now, it was still a giant puzzle.

I drew a line down the middle of the page. On the left side, I wrote "Not suspects" and underneath I put: mother, Amos Walken, and Jim Madison. On the right side under "Suspects," I wrote: Sally? Clint Madden? Unknown male caller? Stranger? And at the top of the page I added "Lacey Walken," and I drew a circle around the two words.

I chewed the tip of my pencil. Maybe I should just make one big list and cross the names off later? I had to find a motive. If it was Sally, why would she kill Lacey? Was she jealous of her? Did Lacey come between her and a boyfriend of hers? But it didn't make practical sense for Sally to do this; after all, Lacey was paying half of the rent and everything else.

The next name, Clint Madden, was a mystery. I had come across his name in the articles, and he may have been the last person to see her that night when she left work. I pulled out my laptop and did a search. Several names popped up. I added a few choice words: Clint Madden, pizza, manager, food industry, Carlton, and Murder Creek. I didn't think I'd find anything this narrow, but what the heck? No harm in trying. I skipped a bunch of discombobulated "Clints" and "Maddens."

I saw a line in the search list with his name, so I clicked. Out popped a small article. I had assumed a guy this hog-wild over his newfound fame was bound to do it again. And I was right; he even mentioned his previous role in the pizza joint, as if it was an *entrée* to his being famous. Was he an idiot, a knucklehead? Or was he a clever criminal mentioning the deed in the open, as if it would assure his innocence in a crime?

I scrolled through the article slowly, so as not to miss anything. This one was about a robbery in front of a store, and Clint provided eyewitness statements. He emerged as a hero, having acted fast, snatching the purse from the thief before the old woman could recover from her shock. There he was, a picture of a smiling Clint with the woman, her purse front and center of the camera. And the unfortunate thug? Well, it seemed he had escaped in all the ruckus. Clint was the good guy, champion of women victims. I came across the next article. The MO was strikingly familiar. Another robbery, inside a diner this time. The thief dashing out and the man chasing him, tackling him and wrestling the backpack from him. The man, Clint, bowing to the applause of the onlookers as he presented the backpack to the young woman. Another little write-up with a picture.

Was Clint in the right place and right time in each robbery? I wondered.

The waitress set my plate on the table as I hurried to clear a spot. She glanced at the photos and papers.

I couldn't resist asking her, "Did you know Lacey?"

She shook her head. I dug into my food, everything forgotten for now except my dinner.

Chapter 29

SOMETIMES I GET ideas when I'm in the shower, or walking, or when I'm doing anything but thinking about a problem when I've run into a brick wall. That's when unbidden thoughts have snuck in.

What if I was going about this all wrong? Was I missing something right in front of me? I felt I was making progress, but slowly. Perhaps there was another connection to Murder Creek.

I pushed away the growing stack of papers and my scribbled notes. Just pieces of a puzzle. I had to figure it out and piece it together. I could be patient when I wanted to be. Lacey had been missing for years. Could new information surface now? Or was her trail too cold?

I stirred another packet of sugar in my coffee. The clinking of the spoon was a welcome and familiar sound. It was Saturday. I'd been here since Wednesday afternoon. Sooner rather than later, I'd have to go back to the city and work. I needed to talk to Jeremy Madison tomorrow. I got a few leads on where to find Clint Madden, and some numbers to call.

The waitress came by to check on me, topping off my coffee cup without asking me. I noticed her name tag, Darlene, as she leaned over. The place had cleared out a bit by now.

"What would you do, Darlene?" I asked her.

She gave me a sympathetic look. I'm sure she had coddled many an upset, tipsy, or rowdy customer, and charmed others.

"Hey, hon, it'll make sense."

"I haven't figured it out yet, but I will. I've got to write my paper."

"Just write what you know," said Darlene, giving me a wink. "It'll all work out."

I heard a text arrive on my phone. Mike Deen.

Seconds later, my phone rang. Apparently, Mike was never one to wait for a text back. I pictured him impatiently tapping his fingers. I took the call.

"Hey, Mike, what's going on?"

"How's your research?"

I laughed. "You should see me pulling my hair out."

"That bad?"

"I don't know if I'll find anything new about Lacey." I wanted so desperately to make some sense out of all this, or uncover a new clue. "You know everyone in town, Mike. How about introducing me to more people who knew Lacey?"

"Well, people have moved on, or passed away. It's been so many years."

"I've got to run," I said abruptly. I'd just had a thought.

I needed to ask Mrs. Walken about Lacey's missing persons files and if I could see her old room or her stuff. She was Lacey's mother, her next of kin.

Chapter 30

TOMORROW I'D HAVE my work cut out for me. I went back to my motel room to shower and to get a good night's sleep. As my head touched the pillow, I found myself back at Murder Creek. Back in the 1800s. In the same scene, before the murders occurred. These men, offering to share their food with a group of strangers, having a meal together. Their last meal.

The young sandy-haired guy was speaking, laughing at someone's joke. Their guard was down. They had warm food in their bellies and were getting ready to settle down for the night. The others, the group of strangers, retreated to another area close by.

The main group stayed by the tree overlooking the creek. They were headed back south to their families from Georgia. After gold was found in north Georgia in late 1828, the Georgia Gold Rush was on with the discovery of the Dahlonega Gold Belt in 1829. It didn't pan out for some, but they had been lucky. Maybe it was more than luck, just the sheer determination to put everything they had into it.

The adventurous eager-eyed youngsters learned quickly and worked together and adapted. The fittest survived. They were careful to hide their gold. For along with the gold miners came the bandits and robbers.

I tried to fall asleep, but the images of the men at Murder Creek reappeared; they sat around a campfire; the flames flickering as the dusk settled. The men eating together, fellow travelers sharing their food. Greed, betrayal, bloody violence, and death. There wasn't any way to warn these men.

I tossed and turned increasingly in futility, wanting to alert them, to shout out before it was too late—before they were murdered in their sleep. Exhausted, I finally sank back down on my pillow as my eyelids grew heavier, even as I became more distraught, deliriously mouthing, "No, no! Get up, don't fall asleep!"

Chapter 31

I WENT BACK to talk to Lacey's mother. This time I didn't call ahead. I just knocked on the front door.

She looked surprised. I wasn't sure how glad she was to see me again.

"I couldn't sleep last night," I said. It was true, but not the real reason I came. I looked for empathy and thought I saw a glimpse.

We stood there. She didn't ask me in. "Is there something I can help you with?"

"Well, I was just thinking, and seeing as I was in the neighborhood, I thought I'd stop by again," I said politely. "To ask about Lacey."

She held the screen door open, but still didn't invite me inside.

"I'd like to see what files you have on Lacey's disappearance," I said.

"What files?"

"You know, on her disappearance—I mean, the investigation."

"Why are you asking me?"

"Seeing you're her mother and all …" I stopped before any tone of accusation crept in. Could she have been involved in her daughter's disappearance? And I didn't want to kill her hopes of finding Lacey alive. However, I was beginning to wonder. Was she hiding anything? And if so, why?

"Mrs. Walken, I've been down to the sheriff's office, but they can't release the files to me. So I was wondering if they had shared them with you, perhaps?"

She really would not budge. "I'm afraid I can't help you there."

I forced a smile to hide my disappointment. You know honey attracts bees and all. "Perhaps I can see some of Lacey's things, you know, to get to know her better?"

She shook her head. "She didn't leave all that much behind when she left." I detected a note of bitterness.

"I'm sorry to have bothered you, ma'am," I said. "But if you think of anything else or have something of hers to show me, please call me."

Chapter 32

"HAVING A BAD day?" The motel clerk took one look at my face and knew.

My crappy, sour look. I was pissed. I dragged myself back to the motel to check on room availabilities.

"It's too early to say, isn't it?" I answered without hissing at him.

"What can I help you with today?"

"You wouldn't happen to know where to find Clint Madden, would you?" I asked, as his name popped up first. I would go down my list until I got to a name he knew.

He looked startled, but quickly gathered his composure and coughed delicately.

Bingo!

"Clint Madden," I repeated, sure this time. I was like a fisherman ready to reel in a catch. "You know him," I said, more of a statement rather than a question. Something told me the clerk's reaction was not normal.

He snorted. "Who wouldn't know a pompous ass when you see one?"

"So I take it you aren't friends?"

"Hell no," he said emphatically. "Shit, that man would rob me of my last nickel and dime."

"How do you mean?"

"Well, me and him, we used to hang out together. Not real tight, but you know." He looked at me to see if I knew what he meant.

"Go on," I said.

"He came to me with this sob story, like he was down on his luck with nobody to turn to, and could I lend him a hand?"

"Did he want money?"

"Heck yeah. I didn't have much, but he swore up and down he just wanna borrow the money, and he'd return it to me."

I had a feeling what was coming up, and it didn't sit right with me. "So you lent him some money."

"Yep, fifty bucks." He shook his head. "It may not be a lot to you, but it was to me."

"I'm sorry," I said, thinking he never got it back. "And he never …"

"Nope."

I leaned against the counter, getting chummy and real friendly. I looked him in the eyes and then glanced down at his shirt, searching for a name tag but finding none. "Look, uh," I mumbled. "Uh … what's your name?"

"Randy."

"Yeah, Randy," I said. "Man, that sucks." I shook my head and gave him a sympathetic look.

"You know, I thought he was my friend."

"When was the last time you saw him?"

"After the news died down about Lacey, he left town I guess," Randy said.

"And you haven't seen him since?"

"Nah."

"Did he ever talk to you about Lacey?"

"Not much. I mean, he mentioned helping her when she got a job at the pizza place. You know, showing her the ropes and all."

"Was he the manager then?"

Randy frowned in deep thought. "I think it was earlier, but he became the manager." He shrugged. "You know him, he was all about money."

"He got promoted to the manager?"

"I guess. I mean … that was in the news. He and I didn't talk then."

"I see. And you never met Lacey?"

He hesitated, then shook his head. Then he changed the subject real quick, probably hoping I wouldn't notice. But I did.

"You here to pay for another night?"

"Seeing how this is Sunday already, I need to stay at least another couple of nights."

"You're in luck. Our rates are going down," he said, smiling. "You know, after the funeral and all."

"I see," I said, giving a conspiratorial wink. "In that case, I'll stay for three more nights."

Chapter 33

I STOPPED BY the diner to pick up breakfast biscuit sandwiches and fresh-brewed coffee. I sipped my coffee while I waited for my food.

Darlene was busy with the breakfast crowd, but she gave me a wink as she walked by. I felt like today would be my lucky day. I thought, *Heck, I think I'll go to church this morning.* I heard my name called, and I looked up to see a girl holding a paper bag. I walked to the counter, my mouth already salivating, as she handed me the biscuits.

"Would you like a refill?" she said, glancing at my cup.

Her name tag said "Sophie". I looked at her in appreciation. I hadn't seen her before. She was about my age I guessed. "Thanks, that's so sweet of you."

Sophie beamed, filled my cup, then popped on a new lid.

"There you go," she said.

"I haven't seen you here," I said.

"Oh, today's my first day," she said brightly, her enthusiasm bubbling. "I don't know how to use the cash register yet, so they have me helping here."

She grabbed a towel and wiped down the counter. I liked a self-starter, someone who could multitask and keep herself busy.

"Well congratulations," I said. "They're lucky to have you."

She looked like she was ready to squeal if she could. I had made her day.

I was humming as I walked to my car. Five minutes later, I rubbed my buttery fingers on the napkin and smacked my lips.

Everything looked brighter today. The sun was out, warming the inside of the car to just the right temperature. I took a final sip of my coffee, sucking out the last drops.

It was too lovely a day to waste. I stretched as I got out of the car to walk. The church was less than a mile away, an easy hike. At the moment, I envied the easygoing life in a small town. Just one lazy day I'd allowed myself.

I slid in the back pew, not bothering to go back to the motel to change into my little black dress. I was in my comfortable jeans, and I told myself God wouldn't judge me for dressing this way. I relaxed into the pew, joining the chorus in singing praises to the Lord. Actually, I wasn't much of a singer and not that religious. But I was in town, and this was what most folks here did every Sunday. The pastor spoke about life and death, the passing of a beloved member of his congregation, Travis Madison III, and how much he was missed. I narrowed my eyes to see farther up front, recognizing Jim and his brother Jeremy near the front. I didn't see Mike though. And the folks who had to work weren't here.

I felt a tap on my shoulder as I walked out after the service.

"Good morning, Eve."

I turned, basking in Jim's effervescent smile. Jeremy was standing next to him with a slight scowl—or was it a figment of my imagination?

"Hi, Jim," I said, turning up my charm. "And Jeremy, how are you today?"

He muttered a reply which sounded like "yeah," before Jim ribbed him. "Great," he said.

I ventured to ask, "Jeremy, I wonder if you could spare a few minutes to talk?"

He raised his eyebrows. "About?"

"Lacey Walken."

Chapter 34

THIS DAY WOULD get better. I would not let any clouds rain on my day. If Jeremy wasn't up to talking, I was unfazed. I jumped right to the point.

"You knew Lacey."

I knew this, because Jim had told me yesterday. Jeremy was a couple of years older, but he knew her. In fact, he hadn't been immune to her beauty. No one was.

Jeremy glanced away, his eyes fixing on something in the distance. "It was a long time ago."

"I need to know whatever you can tell me about her."

He took a step back, almost bumping into Jim. "I have something to confess." Seeing the alarmed looks on our faces, he added quickly, "Oh, gosh no! I didn't harm Lacey." He held out his hands.

I relaxed. I could see Jim's jaw muscle twitching. Brother or no brother, he was tense.

"Lacey asked me to help," Jeremy said. "She, uh, was having some problems with her mom, and things weren't going well at home." He looked at us, shaking his head. "She wanted to run away, drop out of school."

I watched Jim's face, the look of surprise. "Why did she come to you?"

"I could only guess. Perhaps she didn't want to trouble you," said Jeremy, looking at Jim. "I had to think fast, to talk her out of it. The first thought that popped out was to help get her a part-time job at the pizza joint. I gave her an advance, you know, to help tide things over so she could move out. But I convinced her to stay in school."

I did not understand Jeremy's role in this. "Why the pizza place?"

"Well, Dad owned the place, and I was pretty sure I could convince him to give her a part-time job. It was the only thing I could think of, come up with fast. At least she would have a job."

I could see the logic in that. "You talked to your dad?"

Jeremy nodded. "He had some questions, and he didn't want me to get too involved."

"Did your dad know Lacey?"

"He'd met her. And he knew she was in classes with Jim. I mean, he'd heard us talking about her."

"So he was okay with your plan?"

"Well, he was, but he had some conditions."

"Conditions?" Jim spoke up, surprised.

"First, he wanted Lacey's mom to know this and to reassure her that Lacey would not leave town, so this way at least she'd still be close to her."

"She didn't protest?" I asked, a bit incredulous a mother would agree to a plan that would help her daughter leave home.

Jeremy stared at me. "You didn't know Lacey. Once she's made up her mind, no one could talk her out of it."

"She always had this stubborn streak, and I admired her for it," said Jim. "In some ways, she was also mature beyond her years."

"Okay," I said, knowing that Lacey wasn't all alone. I admired her, as a matter of fact. "So, then what happened?"

"Well, she'd put up a note and asked around at the pizza joint about a room. And Sally offered to let her stay at her place. Sally needed the money and Lacey needed a place," said Jeremy.

"A win-win all around," I said. "Did she have any enemies you know of?"

"Enemies?" Jeremy replied. He looked at Jim.

"I mean, were you aware of any problems she was having? Anyone who would want to do her harm?"

Jeremy spread out his fingers and cracked his knuckles. "I could speak about her finances. She came to me again, sometime later."

I was on alert, feeling I was getting closer to what happened.

"She had initially agreed to pay me back, a bit at a time, from her part-time salary. But when her first checks came, and she realized how little money was left after all the deductions and taxes, well, there wasn't much left," said Jeremy.

I could relate to that. The burden of finances was a problem I'd dealt with in my life. "Then what happened?"

"Lacey had her back to the wall. She asked Sally for more

time to pay her rent. But Sally refused to give her an extension. She turned to me."

"And what did you do?"

Jeremy had the saddest look on his face. "I thought I was doing the right thing. I mean, if she learned the lesson, however hard, maybe she would move back home."

"But you know better than that," said Jim, his anguished tone rising.

"Yes, in hindsight. I was tough on her. I told her she had to pay her loan on time too. I laid down a hard line, and I didn't budge," Jeremy said.

I clenched my hands. What had seemed to be an almost perfect solution had turned to crap. Lacey had been in a hole and digging deeper.

"She gave up on school. At that point, it was the only thing she could do, to work full time at the pizza joint," Jeremy said. "I couldn't talk her out of it. She became a dropout and cut off relationships with kids in her class." He turned pale and looked uncomfortable.

"She became isolated from her family and her circle of friends at school," I said. "And working to pay you back, struggling to make ends meet." I really felt for her.

"Why didn't you come clean and tell me before?" Jim said, angry at his brother.

"Lacey had confided in me. She was going through a difficult time, and I'd promised I wouldn't tell," Jeremy said.

"I wish I had been there more for her," Jim said. "I mean, she was pinned into a bad position, and then it was made worse. You're a businessman, Jeremy. You know the pain of losing money and your life, your friends."

"I can't agree with you more," said Jeremy. "But my hands were tied."

"Your hands? You were the one that tied her. I'm surprised Dad didn't come to her rescue."

"I didn't tell Dad until later, toward the end."

"The end?" I gasped. Did Lacey meet her end?

Chapter 35

I CHOKED. I didn't want to hear any more. What had started out to be a beautiful day had turned gray, ugly gray. It was tragic enough, what happened in Lacey's short life. But *the end* sounded so final. Jeremy left abruptly and didn't say more after our conversation.

I was alone with Jim. "You didn't know?"

"No, not all of it."

"This was a surprise?"

"The last few times we met, I could tell she was tense. Different. The carefree days of our childhood and youth were a distant memory," said Jim. "I thought I could make her feel better, and I did in my way … but it only complicated matters."

I listened to him talk, knowing how he had felt about Lacey.

He gripped my hand. A quick clasp, his eyes moist with tears. All I could do was give Jim a hug. The floodgates opened, and he sobbed uncontrollably, heaving deeply. I felt his grief, his pent-up feelings. I felt sorry for him. I just couldn't do anything for him. I said nothing. I just let him sob—sob his heart out, thinking of the anguish of a lover, a friend. A gap that time could not heal. It had come back to him.

"I'm sorry," I whispered. It was all I could think of to say. I had no words left. I felt sad for Lacey. And I felt his loss, one he held in his heart all these years.

Chapter 36

I DECIDED TO follow the money trail. One place I hadn't looked. Now I wanted to see the business records. "Jim, your dad's business … do you know where the records are kept?"

He looked at me, remnants of tears leaving a trace on his cheeks. "What?" He appeared confused.

"His pizza business records."

"He kept them in his office," Jim said. "He turns over the paper ledger books, financials and receipts to his tax accountant, but keeps the records for maybe seven years." He rubbed his eyes and straightened up. "Why are you asking?"

"I'd like to see them, please," I said.

"I'm not sure we'd even have those. I'd have to check with some people, and my brother, of course."

"I don't mean all the local businesses he owns. I'd like to start with the Pizza GoKing."

Jim scratched his head, his eyes sharper and clearer now. "I'll have to check on it. First thing tomorrow morning, on Monday." His demeanor turned businesslike all of a sudden. I felt him withdraw.

"Okay," I said, attempting to sound casual. I didn't know what else to say. "Let me know what they say." I really didn't know what I was searching for, but the pizza place was looming as an important piece of the puzzle, especially after what I learned from the brothers. I wrote my number on a blank page and tore it off. "Call me tomorrow. I'll come by the office."

"I can't promise when, but you'll hear from me before the day is over," he said.

Fair enough. I figured I'd be able to see the records by Tuesday at the latest. I kept my schedule open for that day, anyway. Meanwhile, I wanted to go back and talk to Sally. But not just yet.

I was finding pieces of who Lacey was, but getting no closer to what happened to her that last day after she got off her shift at midnight—the time between midnight and four in the afternoon the next day, when she was due back to work.

I had one more question for Jim. I touched his arm, and he looked surprised. I had been told my smile could disarm a man. Okay, I just thought it would booster my courage; I hadn't really disarmed any man. "You said you loved Lacey," I said gently. "Do you still miss her?"

He turned his face away.

"Is that why you never married?" I had guessed, but I wanted to hear him say it.

"I can't …"

"You can't what?"

The more he tried to speak, the more agitated he got.

"Look, it's fine," I said. "You don't have to tell me now." I thought Jim was still crying over her. That's some love, after all these years.

Chapter 37

THE CALL HAD finally come. I had left messages for a Clint Madden, actually for two Clints. I didn't know who would call me first. "Hello," I said in my most pleasant, beguiling voice.

"You're looking for me?"

"I'd like to talk to Clint Madden."

"Speaking."

"I will ask a few questions to be sure you're the one I'm looking for," I said as I pulled out a file. I spread the newspaper interviews out on the table in my room.

With the picture of his smiling face in front of me, I asked, "Have you ever been interviewed by newspapers?"

He paused. "What's this really about?"

I detected a hint of caution or confusion. "Lacey Walken, do you know her?"

"Is this some kind of joke?" He snorted. "Look, Eve, or whoever you really are. I thought you were someone else. Don't ever call me again."

I pulled my cell phone away from my ear as his voice rose, then he ended the call.

Must not be the right one, then.

I had scribbled several more numbers on the paper next to his name, with question marks. Wasting no time, I tried again. The second number rang and rang. I expected it to go into voicemail, but it didn't. I snarled and ended the call.

Clint Madden could be anywhere. I hadn't the slightest idea. I chewed on my pencil and frowned. My mother used to ream me out for ruining all the pencils she bought for me. I was the only kid in school who showed up on the first day with a pencil box full of teeth marks on each pencil. Some people chewed gum. I chewed pencils. Even now, I hadn't been able to shake this habit. Sometimes when I'm really stressed, I'll clamp down so hard I can almost taste the lead.

But I wasn't a quitter. I'd work my butt off even harder if I couldn't figure out something. I called every number I had scribbled down, even the ones I'd tried yesterday, but got no answer. It seemed I wasn't getting anywhere, but as I was thinking this, my phone rang.

A man's breezy voice sounded like he'd been running. "Just saw your number pop up as a missed call."

"Oh yes, are you Clint Madden?"

"*The* Clint Madden," he said.

"The one from Murder Creek?"

There was a slight pause. "You read the articles?"

I relaxed and mouthed a silent "Thank you." "Yes, I have them spread out in front of me. I'm doing research on the Lacey Walken disappearance." I was grinning broadly for no one to see.

He whistled long and slow. "Well, I'll be …" He paused.

"Why are you digging that one up? It's been long forgotten."

"I'm doing a project and writing an article. And seeing how you were, um, so prominent in the news, I had to talk to you. Could you tell me a bit about Lacey, how you met her?"

"I was a few years older than Lacey, but not by much, so I didn't really know her from school," he said. "The first time I met her—she blew me away. I mean, she was stunning, the way she walked, her long hair flowing."

"Where … at the pizza place?"

"Yep, she had walked in looking for a job. I was working behind the counter, and I pulled out an application and had her fill it out on the spot."

"Were you the manager?"

"I was the *assistant* manager," he said with a hint of pride.

"She got the job?"

"Started the next day," he said, quickly adding, "After she left, the boss man's son called. I already thought she was someone special, so you know, she got hired right away, anyway."

"And how was she as an employee?"

"Seeing this was her first job and all, I had to teach her the ropes. But she was a quick learner … I heard some people complained I was spending too much time with her, but it was the training."

"Did you fraternize with her outside of work, or was it strictly work-related?"

"Hey, I didn't do nothing wrong. Don't you go pointing fingers at me. She and I got along just fine."

I let it go for now. I'd ask again later. I rustled through the papers, finding the one that showed his smiling face in front of the pizza joint. "It says here in the papers you were the last one to see her that day when her shift ended at midnight."

"That's right. We closed out the place together. I did the register, and we both cleaned up. It was more like almost one in the morning when we walked out."

"Is midnight when you normally close?"

"No, only on weekends. During the week we close earlier, at nine."

"Do you remember what happened next?"

"Like I told the sheriff, we parted ways then. I assumed she went home, and that's where I went."

"Did she say anything, or did you notice anything different?"

He took a moment to answer. I could almost imagine him scrunching his eyes and trying to think. "Now that you mention it, she was quieter than usual. I mean, she wasn't a real chatty type of person, but she'd talk. I could tell she was a bit moody."

"She confided in you?"

"Nah, I didn't pry either."

"Any guesses?"

"Not any I'd like to venture. Look, I've gone over what I know, what's in the newspapers."

"I'm hoping you could help me shed some light on it," I said. "Put this to rest."

"You know she was living with this girl, Sally. Have you talked to her?"

"Yes. Oh, and one more thing, I heard Lacey became full-time. Can you talk about that?"

"It wasn't long after she started. When Lacey became full-time, she quit school."

"What did you think about that?"

"I was happy for her, of course. I had trained her, and I was her boss."

"Did you get promoted?"

"Around that time, yes. The papers quoted me as 'the manager.'"

"I wasn't sure if they meant the assistant manager, or if you had become the manager."

"The manager."

"Where are you now?"

"I'm living in the city, about a two to three-hour drive away."

"Oh, that's close. Maybe we can meet if we need to talk again?" I was thinking I could wrap up my work here and leave on Wednesday.

"Just let me know."

Chapter 38

JIM HAD LEFT me a text while I was talking, letting me know I could come by and see the books. The morning kept getting better. Jim gave me the address to Travis Madison's residence. That was where his dad had his office. I stopped by the diner to grab a sandwich.

To call it impressive would be an understatement. The home was a downsized miniature version of a mansion, surrounded by a lush green manicured lawn, trimmed hedges, and colorful flowers, and rimmed by a fence. As the gate opened, I drove up the circular driveway.

Jim was waiting for me, the front door partly opened. I clutched my lunch bag, slung the backpack over my shoulder, and scooted out of my car. I basked in the sight of the beautifully landscaped lawn and inhaled a deep breath, smelling the fresh air tinged with nature's perfume.

"You made it. Please come in," said Jim, greeting me warmly.

He held the door open and gestured for me to come inside. The entryway was every bit as impressive with a spiral staircase winding its way up, disappearing above the tall ceiling. It was quiet. The curtains were pulled back, the rooms bright with sunlight beaming in.

"Would you like a tour?"

I jumped at the offer and followed Jim as he regaled me with the history of the house. He pointed out the details of the workmanship where his dad had insisted on the best, importing the finest marble from Italy, shale for the fireplace, and tiles from France. His dad had been involved with every aspect of the planning and design.

Standing in this man's passionate masterpiece, I felt a lingering trace of his presence, and a sadness.

Chapter 39

WE WALKED OUT to the garden and sat in the gazebo. I ate my lunch outside amongst the busy bees and the canvas of colorful flowers, enjoying the gentle breeze.

"This was his idea," said Jim.

"Hmm?" I mumbled, my mouth full of the egg salad sandwich.

"The gazebo. He hired an architect to design and build it." Jim pointed to the features on the ceiling and the carving on the lattice piece around it. "Every detail. He had an eye for beauty."

"I wish I had a chance to meet him," I said, then almost regretted saying it.

"Well, he was just like everybody else. He had his good side and bad. And he had something else—his greatness," said Jim. He spoke in a low voice as he reminisced. "He raised us with an iron hand. We were his children, but he expected more from us, more than the magnificent pieces he created."

I paused as I took the last bite and finished my sandwich. "But you loved him?"

"Yes, but I also hated him," Jim said, not with meanness, but with the clarity of a man who had chosen his words and spoken the truth.

"I'm sorry for your pain."

"Let's go inside, shall we?" Jim said abruptly, standing up. I gathered my things and followed him inside to his father's office.

On an ornate, massive wooden desk, two books had been laid out next to a small stack of papers. Jim pointed to them. "The Pizza GoKing closed shortly after Lacey's disappearance. My dad kept just the last year's set of books on the business. He was an old-fashioned guy and preferred the paper ledger books. You'll find sales, orders, and payroll information there. Please have a seat and let me know if there's anything else you need."

I made myself comfortable and took out my notepad and pencil, ready to plunge in. I checked the time, and it was already half-past one in the afternoon. I hunkered down and got to work, opening the first book. I glanced through it, scanning the dates, the last twelve months of entries. I quickly picked up the second book, going through the entries until I got to the date they hired her, the day after Lacey first walked through the door of Pizza GoKing. It was there: her starting salary, her hours, and her first pay. I scribbled that down in my notebook and looked for the next notation on her change to full-time hours. I made a note of her new salary, the hours, and her pay. It was more than double her starting salary. What Clint said, I verified it.

I picked up the papers neatly stacked in a small pile; the

timesheets from the last month. I flipped the pages to find the last week Lacey had worked. I ran my fingers slowly down the columns to find Lacey's time in, time out, and number of hours. She had worked an eight-hour shift from four in the afternoon to midnight the weekend before. My finger quivered as I located the entries on her last day. I stopped, taking a breath before I looked at Lacey's timesheet on the last day she had worked.

Lacey didn't work the full eight-hour shift that night. She had left early—two hours before her shift ended.

Chapter 40

I HAD TALKED to Clint, and he'd smoothly answered all my questions, and deflected and pointed fingers at Sally. Granted, I didn't get warm fuzzy feelers when I talked to Sally, but Clint had sounded so convincing. I grabbed my backpack and rummaged through to find his file.

I quickly spread out the articles on the desk and scanned them, looking for when Lacey last worked. It was there. They reported the last shift she worked was the evening shift, the four to midnight. I reread the stories carefully, especially where Clint had been quoted. Crap! I had assumed she worked to midnight, but it was mentioned only in reference to the shift. There was nothing in print she left prior to midnight before her shift ended. I got up, pacing the floor. I walked up to the window and looked out across the lawn, seeing the gazebo and the lovely view. I had found this two-hour aberration to my original timeline. Lacey had left early. I wondered why Clint lied. Suddenly I could not wait to go back to the city. I had to see him and get some answers. But I also needed to talk to Sally again.

I closed the book, and I wandered out to the hallway, looking for Jim. He was sitting in the front room, waiting for me.

"Find what you needed?" he asked.

I nodded. "Listen, thank you for your help," I said, fumbling for my car keys. "I'm leaving town tomorrow."

"Will you be back?"

I licked my lips. "I plan to."

Chapter 41

I DROVE BACK to the motel and made my way to the front lobby, hoping to see Randy. I wondered if he lived onsite. I didn't see him at the counter. I dinged the bell. To my relief, the back door opened, and he stepped out.

"What can I help you with?" Randy said, easing into his chair.

"I'd like to leave a day early. I paid for three nights, Sunday through Tuesday, leaving Wednesday. I'd like to leave on Tuesday instead."

Randy turned on the computer and checked. "I can make the change. Will you be coming back?"

"I think I may come back for a short stay, but I don't know for sure yet."

"When you check out tomorrow, I'll give you the refund."

I mumbled, "Thank you" and went to my room. I threw my backpack on the table and sprawled on the bed, arms wide, looking at the ceiling. In my heart of hearts, I felt I was getting closer to the truth. I was getting to know Lacey too.

I felt for her, what she struggled with. What could have made her leave work early? Why did Clint lie to me? Did he think I'd just go along with what he said and what was reported, and not question it?

I closed my eyes and dozed off as the afternoon sun warmed the windows. The image of Murder Creek returned as my eyelids fluttered. I saw the men sitting around a campfire. I heard the crackling as flames licked and danced. It was darker, night already, no longer dusk. The stars were peeking out. I couldn't see the creek, but I could hear the faint sound of water flowing. The men were laughing; some drank, others stretched out, their stomachs full of food.

I saw the group of men sitting with the strangers who had joined them. They were talking. Soon, one of the visitors got up, said something to the others; the strangers made ready to leave. The men got ready for bed, sleeping under the tree and around the fire, using their saddlebags as pillows.

I tossed in my sleep, flinging my arms to the left and to the right, frantically trying to touch the men, to warn them. I kicked out, aiming at their outstretched legs as they lay down. I couldn't seem to touch them. I screamed, yelling until my lungs felt like they'd burst. *Please wake up.* I was crying now, pleading with them to wake up. My tears streamed down as I kneeled in front of each man, helpless as I watched the drops land on their faces and chest, to no avail.

A fright seized my chest as I huffed and heaved. I knew what would happen, yet I could do nothing to save them from the group of strangers who would brutally murder them in their sleep, leaving a bloody carnage. I glanced at the young sandy-haired kid, barely a man, soon to be robbed of his life ahead.

I woke up, finding my whole body on top of the bed covers, the sheets twisted around me, my legs entangled. My pillow teetered on the edge of the bed, about to fall on the floor. I sat up, rubbing my eyes. I was in my motel room, the late afternoon sun still coming through the solitary window. I shivered, my body convulsing.

I freed my legs, got up, and stumbled to the bathroom. Bending over the sink, I peered in the mirror. I looked like hell. My eyes were red, puffed, and swollen. The folds of the sheets had dug into my cheeks, creating a pattern of crisscrossing lines. I splashed cold water on my face, not waiting for the temperature to warm.

My body ached. The feeling I had *been* there with the men was stronger than ever before.

Chapter 42

SALLY WASN'T HOME. I walked around her yard, the tiny piece of green posing as her front lawn. It was a far cry from the grandeur of the Madison mansion. I kicked an empty beer can in the yard, probably tossed there by someone driving or walking by. A piece of tissue fluttered, carried by a gentle breeze before it settled on the grass. Weeds had pushed their way between the cracks of the walkway and the steps of her front porch.

I looked around her neighborhood. It was quiet this time of the day. I felt the perspiration trickle down my face. Hot and humid. With nothing else on my mind, I walked down the road, kicking up dust from the gravel.

I could see the railroad tracks were about a hundred feet away. It was close. I shuddered to think how thunderously loud it would be when the train whizzed by, rocking the foundations of the homes so close to it.

It wasn't long before I ran into two little boys playing by the tracks. My heart beat faster. I rushed over to them. "You're too close to the tracks."

One boy, a scrawny kid with a trace of snot smeared across his nose, looked up at me unfazed. "There ain't no trains coming now."

"Do you know how fast they come?" I said as my breaths came in huffs. "Didn't anyone tell you not to play on the tracks?"

The other boy who was shorter stood up now, watching the two of us.

"You're not my mother."

"Kid, what's your name?" I hissed.

"Me, I'm Joey," he said. Tossing his head toward the taller boy, he said, "And this here's Tommy."

I calmed down. "I'm Eve, glad to make your acquaintance." I extended my hand for a shake.

Joey pumped my hand with quick energy. I shook Tommy's hand next. He barely touched mine, and it fell limp as soon as I let go.

"You kids live around here?"

"Over yonder," said Joey, pointing to a ramshackle house down the road.

"What do you like to do around here?"

Joey shrugged his thin shoulders. "We play ball, and we hang around the railroad."

"Look, I'm sorry to have yelled at you, but the railroad tracks are a dangerous place," I said.

"It don't come around at this time," said Joey.

"So, when does it come?"

"Oh, real late at night and in the mornings."

"Does it wake you up?"

He shook his head. "I'm used to it. I sleep through it."

"Well, you boys be careful now, will you?" I asked. "Promise me?"

Joey grinned. I could see the merriment in his eyes, probably over the fuss I made over them.

I asked them if they knew Sally, pointing to her house.

They looked at each other, then made yucky faces.

I raised my eyebrows as if to say, *So what did you think?* "Do you know when she gets home?"

They shook their heads. Joey said, "She's a mean one."

"What does she do?"

"She chases us if she catches us on her porch or in her yard. Thinks we're gonna do somethin' bad, I guess."

"But why is she so mean?"

"I don't know," said Joey, shrugging. "But they say something happened to her." He made a circle with his finger around his head.

"You mean loco?"

"Uh, huh."

I hadn't heard. I mean, maybe she drank too much, but she didn't sound or act crazy when she was talking to me.

"She doesn't like kids," said Joey.

"Or any of us," Tommy added.

"That's no reason to call someone names. Some people just plain don't like kids. Well, I best be going. You kids watch yourselves and stay off the track," I said again, looking as stern as I could. I wasn't old enough to be their mother, but maybe their older sister.

I parted ways and walked back to Sally's house, turning

around once to see if they were still there. By then, they had left and were on their way home. I sighed with relief.

I trudged up the steps to Sally's porch once more and again knocked on her door. Hearing no response, I turned around and left.

Chapter 43

I WOKE UP before my alarm went off. Maybe I didn't rest easy, or I was feeling anxious about leaving and going back to the city to talk to Clint. I called Mike to give him a quick update and let him know I was leaving. I didn't mention the part about Clint or what I came across on Lacey's work records.

There wasn't much to pack. I threw my clothes, backpack, and pocketbook in the car and checked out of the motel in no time at all.

The drive back to the city was uneventful. I made it without stopping except for once. I had left a message for Clint inviting him for lunch, and he called me back right away. He had suspected nothing. I didn't have any plans yet on what I'd say when I saw him.

I made good time and arrived early. Clint had chosen a quirky Salvadorian place that served savory home-cooked meals. The place was colorfully decorated with dyed handwoven fabrics and paintings. Latin American music played over the speakers. Clint introduced me to the menu, and the bilingual waitstaff quickly took our orders. He had the lunch special, steak with onions, *Bistec Encebollado*. I ordered the fried plantains and beans, *Platano Frito con Crema y Frijoles*, with a side of rice. We both had a pink, fruity drink.

The food was delicious, and I became full quickly. It was a good choice. Living in the city had its pluses, and authentic ethnic food was one of them. I watched as Clint cut the last piece of his greasy steak and wolfed it down while I sipped my drink.

He finally finished, wiped his mouth with the napkin, and threw it on the table.

"Great suggestion, Clint," I said.

"I couldn't turn down lunch with a lovely lady," Clint said, all charm. He had aged some compared to his looks in the newspaper clippings. He'd gained some weight and the jowl on his chin jiggled as he chewed. But his personality was bubbly.

"Thank you for coming," I said, pushing my plate out of the way as I dug into my backpack and pulled out the newspaper articles. "I'm glad we talked yesterday."

He leaned closer to look at—no, rather to admire—the articles, pointing to one with a very flattering photo of him. "Man, I haven't seen these in years." He grinned so broadly I could see the gum line of his teeth.

"These are preserved in the annals of newspaper history," I said seriously. I sat back, watching as he took his time reading them, wearing an expression of delight and awe as he admired himself in each one. By the time he was done, he was grinning nonstop.

"May I?" He was holding the stack against his chest, reluctant to return them.

"Why don't I make you a copy after we leave?" I said graciously. I fluffed his feathers and watched him puff out more. I could tell he was elated. I gently tugged the papers out of his hands.

His eyes traveled with them, watching me put them back into the folder. "Don't worry," I said, patting the folder. "They're all safe here."

He relaxed and leaned back in his chair.

"You said after you and Lacey left the pizza place at about one in the morning, then you went your separate ways?"

"That's right."

"Did you ever see Lacey again after that?"

"Nope."

"That was the last time?"

He nodded. "If I had known it would be the last time, I would have done something." His voice trembled. I couldn't tell if he was a good actor or sincere.

"Did Lacey have any enemies, anyone who would want to harm her?"

He thought for a moment. "Well, I don't know if I should say this," he ventured, then hesitated.

"Go ahead."

He lowered his voice. "I overheard a conversation at the pizza place once. She and Sally were talking. Rather, it seemed like they were arguing." Then Clint got apologetic. "I mean, I wasn't listening or spying on them. They were talking so loud I couldn't help overhearing."

"What was the argument about?"

"From what I heard, they mentioned money."

I knew Lacey was paying rent to Sally, so I wasn't surprised. "Anything else?" I said, trying to sound excited and interested.

"Well, they were talking about someone else, a guy."

My ears perked up. Hmm, arguing about a guy. This could be real interesting. "Who was it?"

"One of the Madison boys, but I couldn't be sure if it was Jeremy or James."

"I see." But that didn't explain why he lied to me. Okay, time to confront him.

"You know, I spoke to the Madison boys earlier."

He raised his eyebrows.

I went on easily, "Travis Madison III died. I was at the funeral."

Now Clint looked surprised.

I twirled my pencil, watching it spin on the tablecloth. "Are you positive Lacey worked with you the entire shift to midnight?"

He squirmed in his chair and cleared his throat before he whispered. "Sure I am."

"If not, you could be an accessory to murder," I said calmly as I pierced him with a steely gaze.

"Murder? That's absurd," he mumbled. "Lacey's body has never been found. She's missing."

"I believe it's just a matter of time," I said confidently.

He was silent.

"You knew she left early that night, didn't you? Yet you

covered that up," I said.

Clint shook his head.

I pressed him, "You lied, because you knew whoever she left early to meet was the killer, didn't you?"

"Oh no, no." He cried out, shoulders trembling. "Please don't."

"Even if you didn't know who, you lied to cover this up. And you lied about her timeline." I pressed on, pushing him hard.

"I'm sorry," said Clint, looking panicky.

I glared at him. "You'd better come clean—now."

Clint looked resigned, taking a breath before exhaling slowly. "I had to lie back then. I got a phone call … heard a muffled voice, a guy's. He said for me not to tell anyone she left early."

"He threatened you?"

"Well, not exactly. I asked what's in it for me, and he said five hundred bucks cash."

"So he bribed you."

"I … I took the money—but that was before I found out she went missing."

"And you've regretted it ever since?"

"It was blood money, tainted," he whispered.

Somebody went to the trouble of luring Lacey out and making sure no one knew she left early. How could I know if Clint was telling the truth this time? I was irritated at him, at his sniveling face and dishonesty.

"Clint, when did you realize Lacey was missing?"

"The next day when she didn't show up for work. I called

around looking for her and talked to her roommate. Sally didn't know where she was."

"Had she seen her?"

"Not from what she told me."

"Do you have anything else to tell me?"

"Just find poor Lacey and get us all some peace."

Clint sounded sincere at this point.

"If you remember anything else that night … well, you have my number. Call me."

Chapter 44

MY PHONE WAS on silent during our lunch. Leaving the restaurant, I checked my messages. I had one from a number I didn't recognize, so I called back.

"Hello," a female voice answered.

"Hi, this is Eve Sawyer calling you back. Who's this?"

"I'd rather not say. I saw your ad in the newspaper. I have some information for you."

"I'm walking to my car, just give me a second." I closed the driver's door and grabbed my notepad and pencil. "Okay, I'm all ears."

"Well, we got to talking, with what's going on with the funeral and all …"

"We?"

"Me and my boyfriend, Randy, and he was talking about old man Travis and all, and Lacey. I thought, what's he talking about?"

I gripped my phone, holding it closer to my ear.

"He let slip he heard Travis had somethin' to do with it."

I gulped, keeping my voice down. "Do … with what?"

"It just didn't sit right with me." She paused. "He said somethin' like the old man was afraid Lacey was going to spill the beans."

My heart thumped faster, beating rapidly against my chest.

"What did he do, the old man?" I whispered. "Did he … kill her?"

"Randy said he paid someone big bucks to scare her off."

"Did he say who?"

"Travis was drunk, but he said nothin' about who it was."

"How?" I stuttered, feeling my stomach knot up. "Did he hurt her?"

"He, ugh … beat her up."

I gulped, my trembling fingers turning white as they gripped the phone. "He roughed her up a little?"

She paused at the other end. A *long* pause.

"He messed up her face real bad. Then he delivered the message to Lacey to leave town and never come back."

Chapter 45

AFTER THE CALL, I sat in my car feeling numb, my body frozen. I clutched my backpack tightly to my chest.

I couldn't still my thoughts; they were swirling like mad. The old man was dead. *He* did that to Lacey. But was she still alive?

I didn't know how long I stayed still, stuck in the driver's seat, my muscles stiffened. I finally started my car, and I headed back to Murder Creek immediately. My mind was working on overdrive, putting the pieces together.

Lacey wouldn't have left work unless it was somebody she knew. Who had betrayed her?

It was late afternoon when I arrived in town. I had called ahead and asked Jeremy to meet me. He sounded surprised I was back so soon.

We met at the church parking lot. It was Tuesday afternoon and quiet. Jeremy was already there when I pulled up. He was pacing back and forth. As soon as he saw me, he rushed up to my car.

"Are you okay?" he asked.

I waved him off and got right to the point.

"Jeremy, the last night Lacey worked, did you talk to her?"

He blurted, "I had talked to her earlier in the day, before her evening shift." He frowned. "What's this about?"

"She got a call from somebody she knew that evening. It wasn't you?"

"No, I didn't call her at work."

I knew where I had to go next. There was someone else she trusted.

I drove to the mansion to see Jim. He met me at the circular driveway, but this time he didn't usher me into the house.

"How about we sit and talk?" I said.

He gestured to the chairs on the porch "Back so soon?" he asked, running his fingers through his hair.

"Seems like I overlooked something."

"How can I help you?"

"You called Lacey that night, didn't you? The night before she disappeared."

He turned away, shifting in his seat.

"What did you call her about?"

He worked his jaws, clenching and unclenching his teeth. Then he stopped moving and just stared down with a defeated look on his face—like a child who did something wrong and was caught. Mixed with relief or some weirdness I couldn't make out.

"I called because I wanted to see her," Jim said.

"But she was working and wouldn't have just left."

"I told her it was urgent."

I felt the tingling down my spine and shivered.

"So, she rushed out right away to see you …"

"Yes," he whispered. "To meet at our usual spot at Murder Creek." I had to move closer to catch his whisper. "But it wasn't to do what she thought."

I stared at him, this man who tricked the woman he said he loved.

"And then?"

"Then I left and let Ray Moore do his thing."

I gasped. "The sheriff? So you knew what he'd do?"

He hung his head and looked down at his hands. His whispered "Yes" was almost inaudible.

"And you left her there alone with him?" I felt the sour bile in my throat and I almost threw up. "Why?" I rasped.

He sat there staring at his hands, turning the palms up, then over again. "My old man." He slumped into the chair. "He said he was afraid she'd spill the beans, you know, ruin everything. He wanted to beat her to the punch." He laughed dourly. "So, she got punched."

I snorted, spitting my words out. "But why?"

"You know she moved out of her home," said Jim. "She confided in me, told me why. I told my dad."

"What did it have to do with your dad?"

"Lacey caught him … with her mom … having sex."

I suddenly understood. "So that's why she left home."

"And Lacey had told no one until she confided in me. Dad was still married at the time and had us two kids. He was a pillar of the community, and this would have ruined him."

"She had no idea you'd turn around and betray her."

"I had to, he was my dad," whined Jim. It sounded so unbecoming.

"What, he threatened to punch you too?"

His face flushed, probably with shame. "No, he threatened to cut me out of his will. And this mansion …"

Chapter 46

I WAS STILL shaking after I left the mansion. I drove to the diner, hoping my favorite table would be available. Pushing the door open, the familiar clinking of dishes and silverware and the aroma from the cooking food greeted me. I looked for Darlene, but I didn't see her.

The new waitress, Sophie, waved when she saw me, and she pulled out a menu and a set of rolled silverware in a napkin.

"I'd like that table, please," I said, pointing to my usual spot.

"Of course," she said, leading the way.

I ordered quickly, my usual. "Oh, and please bring me the strongest coffee you've got." As she went to collect my menu, I asked her, "Sophie, do you like working here?"

"I do," she said enthusiastically.

I liked her. "You're doing great," I said.

She brought me my coffee and dinner and left me alone except to refill my cup a few times.

I pulled out my notepad and flipped the pages, reading

as I ate. Everything was falling into place now. All except for one brick.

Lacey had not come to an end here. I now knew the circumstances that forced her to leave. Although not the end of her life, she had faced betrayal, pain, disfigurement, and she had been dealt a cruel and vicious blow. I opened the file folder and picked up the article—the one with her picture— the one that had taken my breath away. Her beauty had haunted me. A teardrop landed on my napkin. My brain didn't register it was mine.

A wave of sadness washed over me. I was helpless to fight it. I couldn't stand up, but wobbled and fell. It tossed and rolled me over. With each surge, another wave came and receded, to be followed by another and another. I lost all track of time as the water sloshed me, pushing and pulling me in the sea. I was dazed, stunned, and the water still came, relentless and strong.

The blue-green of the water suddenly mingled with a brownish tint as I was transported to the gentle gurgling of water flowing over rocks, streaming around bends of lush green grass and wild flowers, and trees with boughs bent over the stream. I stopped struggling and let it take me where it was going. To Murder Creek.

This time it was broad daylight. The sun was shining brightly, and fluffy clouds overhead floated lazily across the blue sky like enormous cotton balls. I was on my back gazing upwards, watching birds fly from treetop to treetop, cawing to each other. I heard the buzzing of insects, their wings flapping energetically. A faint rustling of the grass was a telltale sign of the little critters who moved through the verdant vegetation in the forest, scurrying and foraging for food.

The flowers bobbed their heads as the gentle wind swayed them, their heads and slender stalks flexing in the wind, along with the tall grass.

How peaceful it looked now, the night pushed away by the day. Under the warmth of the sun's rays I felt nourished, reborn, freshly woken up.

I lost track of time. I didn't know how long I had sat there, at my corner table, but I felt relieved knowing why I *didn't* see Lacey's images—only the visions of those men who were murdered. I realized then Lacey didn't suffer the same fate as those murdered men. She *didn't* die at Murder Creek.

I felt the peace and the promise of a new dawn.

Chapter 47

I STIRRED. MY stiff muscles protested. I flexed my arms and twirled my ankles. I clasped my fingers into a ball and unfurled them. I reached for my coffee cup. It felt light. Had I emptied it? Rings of brown inside the cup had almost dried up. I clenched it, holding the cup with both my hands, seeking out the last bit of warmth.

I looked up to catch the attention of Sophie. It was getting late and most of the customers had left. I had lost all track of time.

I saw Sophie walking toward me, a coffee carafe in her hands. *One more cup before I leave*, I said to myself.

"Refill?" Sophie asked.

"Yep, one for the road."

She laughed and poured.

I sat back. As Sophie sat my cup down, her hand trembled. Coffee spilled over the rim and splattered on the table.

"What's wrong?" I asked as I stared at her face. Her eyes transfixed on the newspaper article, Lacey's photo in the center. "Please, let me take the cup," I said, carefully tugging it from her hand.

Her face pale; she looked at the paper again and then at me. I pulled out the chair next to me and sat her down.

I gathered the newspaper articles, to put them away in the folder. "It's a research project I'm doing for my class."

Her hands stopped me. She pried my fingers off and picked up the article.

I sat while she read it slowly. "Lacey Walken," she whispered over and over before she laid it back down on the table.

I raised my eyebrow, waiting for her to speak.

She stared at the photo again.

I cleared my throat. "Yes, that's Lacey Walken," I said, tapping my finger under the caption as if she couldn't read.

She nodded. Wordlessly, she reached for the delicate chain around her neck and pulled out a gold necklace tucked inside her dress.

Chapter 48

"WHAT?" I STUTTERED.

"My mother gave it to me," said Sophie. She opened the locket, showing me the pictures inside.

"Your mother is ... Lacey Walken?" I gasped in shock, repeating it slowly, not trusting the sound of my own voice or the words. I must have stared incredulously.

Lacey's gold necklace. Sophie had it.

"Yes, she's my mother, but she didn't go by Lacey Walken. She had changed it."

I tried again. "Your mother, she's alive?"

"No, she died," Sophie said. Her voice broke.

"When?" I whispered.

"Two months ago. I stayed to make the funeral arrangements and to take care of things. Then I left."

"Your mother, how did she ...?"

"She fell ill and passed."

"I'm so sorry," I said. "Why did you stare at her picture?"

"*Her* picture." Sophie's voice trailed, became flat and distant. "The mother I knew looked nothing like the photo in the newspaper. I had to be sure. The tiny photo in the locket didn't do her justice, but it was all I had of her."

I winced, putting my hands to my cheeks. The men that did this to her, they had messed up her face, ruined her beauty. I reached out to touch Sophie's hand, feeling the softness of youthful skin. I scrutinized her face. She didn't look like her mother, and her hair color was different. She had dark tresses and dark brown eyes. But when I looked closely, I could see she had her mother's exquisite nose and lips. Her chin trembled and her lips quivered, a fresh wound cutting into her mourning.

I pressed her gently. "What did she tell you?"

"My mother said to never, ever let go of this locket. It was the only personal item she left to me."

I gulped.

She paused. "And my mother said, after she died, to go back to Carlton—to Murder Creek."

I rubbed my eyes and blinked, taking all this in. I pushed the folder with her mother's information toward her.

Her eyes were moist, but she held her head high. I sensed an inner strength and resilience in this young girl. I asked to see the locket again.

She pulled it out and popped it open.

I squinted at the photo of the young man, the one facing a young Lacey.

"Do you know this man?" Sophie asked, her lips slightly parted.

I peered closely. It was a tiny photo, and an old one. I stared at the young man, picturing how he might have aged and what he'd look like today. My eyes widened as realization hit me. I stood up, grabbing my phone.

"I'll be right back," I told Sophie, and I rushed out.

Chapter 49

I FINISHED THE brief conversation, asking him to meet me at the diner, saying I'd explain everything when he got here. I had a few minutes and went back to wait.

Meanwhile, Sophie had cleared the table. I didn't have time to explain to her, but from her excited glances my way, I knew she had sensed something was happening. She rushed to finish up with her last customer.

When the door opened, he marched straight toward me. I motioned for him to sit, facing me. His back was to the room.

"I'm so glad you came," I gushed, barely able to contain my excitement.

He gave a throaty laugh. "What's this surprise you mentioned?"

I held up my finger. "Have patience. You'll soon see." I had a view of the room behind him. Sophie was coming toward us, a glass of ice water in one hand.

Sophie sat the water in front of him.

I gestured for her to sit down in the chair beside him.

I couldn't hold back any longer. "Sophie, please show him your gold locket."

She pulled out the chain, fumbling at the catch on the locket.

He reached out. "May I try?"

She leaned forward, stretching the chain and holding the locket in her open hand. As she turned to face him, I watched his reaction.

He frowned, struggling with the clasp, his large hands a contrast to the delicate chain and the small locket.

I wriggled in my seat. I couldn't wait for him to pop it open.

When he finally got it opened, he stared at the photos inside. "Where did you get this?" he said hoarsely. His face ashen, he looked up at Sophie and then turned toward me.

I nudged Sophie. "Meet your dad, Jeremy."

She gave me a bewildered look, eyes questioning. "My dad ... I have a father?"

I turned to Jeremy. "This is your daughter, Sophie."

"Sophie?" said Jeremy in a shaky voice that turned husky. He had the look of someone shell shocked. "I had no idea. This locket ... I had given it to Lacey Walken."

"She was my mother," whispered Sophie with a shy smile. "So this is why my mother sent me to Carlton."

"*Was*?" said Jeremy, a wail escaping from his lips.

I excused myself for a few minutes to give them some privacy, heading toward the women's washroom to dry my own tears.

They were catching up when I returned.

"Mom had kept this secret from me all these years until she was dying, when she gave me this locket. She told me the photos are of her and my dad." Sophie said, rushing her words.

"Why did she keep it a secret?" said Jeremy.

"Mom said it wasn't safe for her to go home to Carlton."

"Did she say why?"

I explained, filling in the parts I knew about Jeremy's father and Lacey's mother. The words tumbled out as I talked about the betrayal and what happened that night at Murder Creek.

Jeremy was clenching his jaw hard. His face turned red, livid with rage. He was furious. Both his father and brother had kept this from him. When I got to the part about Lacey and what they did to her face, he cried out; bawling uncontrollably and sobbing hysterically, his pain and anguish etched on every line of his face.

Sophie was the one to calm him, touching his arm, soothing him.

"You were in love with her," I said softly.

"After she moved out, I helped her. But I didn't tell my father everything. We got to know each other. We fell deeply in love. Lacey mentioned at one time she wasn't sure who to trust."

"Your brother, wasn't he in love with her too?" I had to ask.

"They were friends in school and close, but she wasn't in love with Jim. She said they never took the next step. He wanted to, but she held back." He added, growling, "My brother betrayed her."

146

"But she was in love with you?"

"Yes. We had our photos taken. I had given Lacey the gold locket." He paused. "I told you I talked to Lacey that day before she went missing," said Jeremy. "She …"

I waited, holding my breath.

"We became lovers that morning, for the first time. The *only* time."

Epilogue

I GAVE MARK Sewell my notes. He wrote the story and gave me credit on the byline. The local newspaper published it with the photos of Sophie and her dad front center. The national papers picked it up, and it quickly went global. As for Clint Madden, he got his photo in the newspapers again, much to his delight. Only this time, it was for his donation of five hundred dollars to a women's crime victim fund.

James Madison confessed to giving the anonymous hush money to Clint and fingered Sheriff Ray Moore for the brutal attack on Lacey that disfigured her. I found out later Moore was the anonymous caller who had threatened me. And James Madison? Well, he got what was coming to him, as did the sheriff.

I finished writing my term paper and turned it in to Professor Reynolds. He called me back a few days later. He was a man of few words. But on that day, he praised me.

Three little words. To this day, when life throws me a curve ball, I always remember what he said. "You did good."

Oh, and in case anyone is wondering, I got an A-plus on my report.

I no longer have nightmares about Murder Creek. I still go there to visit occasionally. Drawn to the big tree with its heavy limbs bowing over the creek, I could almost swear there was fresh moisture on the bark, like it had been crying. But it was different now … the tears of relief and peace. And where the drops fell and joined the flowing waters of the creek, the muddied waters now run clear.

I said a prayer for those murdered men. That day on the bridge their tormented souls cried out. Without their deaths, there would be no sign. Without Murder Creek, Lacey would have remained a cold case. As I looked out over the slow-moving peaceful waters, I thanked these men in a silent prayer. They can rest in peace now. I owed it to them for Lacey: for getting her what she deserved to have—truth and justice.

Made in the USA
Las Vegas, NV
07 February 2021

17386240R00094